The Moleskin Cap

M. R. Williamson

WolfSinger Publications ❮ Security, Colorado

Author's Note

I would like to thank and give credit to Terri Pray for her work in editing this work.

I would also like to thank my sister Tammy Barr for the cover photo taken on Elk Mountain.

Part One
The Moleskin Cap

Helen Durkin sat quietly on the back porch of her grandparent's home in Wendover Woods of Mid-Southern England. Twisting her long, blonde hair around her right index finger, she watched the forests around their old home. The majority of her eighteen years had been spent in London with her parent's. But after her mother died of cancer two years ago, the woods and its wild things around the little cottage had become a calming balm to her soul no medicine could ever match.

"Don't wander off now." Her grandmother looked from the partially open kitchen window. "I just put the rolls in and when they brown we'll have supper."

"Yes, Grandma."

Helen's smile widened as she looked through the open window at her grandmother's expression. It was one of those *don't get into anything* looks.

Narbie Tucker had always been there for Helen, especially during the last two years. Now, the forests of Waltham and her mother's parents were all she ever thought of—that is except her mother's SLR Nikon camera. She always had it with her. Now, with the scent of fresh-cut hay in the air, she closed her eyes and leaned back in the old rocker. As she was about to doze off, the sharp chatter of a bird broke the silence.

Goshawk? Strange to see one in this part of the wood.

She eased her hand to the camera sitting on the little table next to her chair. Raising it up, she focused the zoom in on a high, jiggling limb at the lower edge of the back yard. Spotting the brown and white bandit was no problem. His bright flashing, grey banded tail was like a beacon in the shadows. One snap and she had him.

Haven't seen one of you in a while. But what are you fussing at?

Lowering the zoom to just beneath the hawk, she used it to search through the goldenrods and thistles.

"There you are," she said softly, noting the flash of dark brown fur in the scrub.

With at least forty yards between them, she knew this shot wasn't going to be as easy as the little weasel-like bandit. Giving up on the distance, she crept from the east side of the porch.

Let's see how shy you are.

Slipping from the yard and into the woods, she brought the camera up again and checked the goldenrods. They were still moving back and forth, but she still couldn't see the creature.

I'll flank him.

With the chatter of the finches and the still fussing goshawk in the background, she hoped her target would be none the wiser to her presence. A warm, September breeze wisped about her face as she crept to a weak stone's throw from the goldenrods. But now, there was nothing to be seen on the ground. Even the hawk had grown silent.

Strange.

She knelt next to a little spruce and watched patiently. After about ten minutes or so, she had just about given up when someone from behind her spoke.

"Human girls are easy."

The voice was soft a quiet. Whoever it was sounded as old as her Grandfather Martin.

Helen spun around so fast she all but dropped the camera. "Who are you?" she blurted out.

Silence

Helen slowly stood, but the extra height did nothing to help her put a face to the voice.

"Hello," she said timidly again. "I heard you…I know I did."

Still, there came no reply.

"Helen," called Narbie from the back porch. "Helen!" The cry louder this time.

"That certainly wasn't who I heard," grumbled Helen.

She carefully backed out of the goldenrods and into the lower edge of the back yard. As she did, something moved not far in front of her and it wasn't a shadow.

"No-it's-not," she said, letting her chin drop slightly.

There, in the shadows next to a spruce sapling, stood a little silhouette all of three feet tall. It tipped its floppy cap, turned, and then walked toward the darker shadows just passed the spruce. Helen stood there as still as a stump, completely ignorant of the Nikon in her left hand. Then, finally she raised the camera, focused the zoom, and then snapped the shutter as fast as she could work the thumb crank. With her target finally gone, she lowered the camera, backed up a bit, and then trotted toward the cabin.

"I wish you wouldn't ignore me, Helen," complained Narbie.

Helen turned to see her holding the back door open with a disgruntled look.

"Martin's already at the table and laughing at your antics. What has captivated your attention now?" Her grandmother waited patiently for an answer as she dried her hands on her apron and straightened the snood holding the little salt and pepper colored bun on the back of her head.

"Grandmother…" Helen hesitated, wondering what to say to keep from sounding foolish.

"Yes, dear," prompted Narbie as she held the door open.

Helen slowed just inside the doorway, stepped into the kitchen, and then looked at Narbie. "Grandfather knows just about everything that breathes or grows in these woods, doesn't he?" she finally asked.

"Yes, dear. He's been a botanist and a naturalist for as long as I've known him. Just what did you find this time?"

"I think this thing found me," Helen all but whispered. "Does Grandfather still use his dark room?"

"From time to time," replied her grandfather as they stepped into the kitchen.

Martin resembled Mr. McGoo, complete with the required squint, but that and his wire-rimmed glasses didn't fool the people who lived in and around Waltham Forest. Even though his hair was thin as corn silk and he walked with a bit of a wobble, he was still considered one of their sharpest minds.

Helen turned to her grandfather, "I've got a picture of something, grandfather and…and…it spoke to me just before I took it."

Martin's eyebrows raised as he looked at her over his glasses. "Spoke to you did it?" he echoed with a bit of a chuckle. "What did it say?"

"I'd rather not say." Helen lowered her head.

"Helen," Narbie explained with a slight smile, "these old woods will work their magic on a young mind like yours just like alcohol on an old fool."

Martin rolled his eyes and then looked back at the still warm rolls in the basket on the dinner table.

"Maybe so." Helen held up the Nikon. "But this young mind has pictures."

"After supper," said Narbie. "Those pork chops and chips are best when they're hot."

~ * ~

After supper Martin and Helen stood over the developing pans, moving the prints pack and forth in the solution.

"The butterfly is nice," replied Martin as he handed the picture to Helen for the drying line. "Good. You've got a prize here in this hawk moth." Helen pinned the picture on the line as her grandfather fiddled with the goshawk. "This fellow seems to fuss at me at least once a week," he added with a smile. "I think he's drumming up the courage to try one of Narbie's smaller hens."

She moved closer to her grandfather's side. "What about the last four?"

"Can't figure them out," responded Martin as he pushed them under the solution again. "I don't think that zoom helped you at all in the shadows of the forest. But, all in all, I do think you've got something here even if it is just a hint in a shadow."

Martin then picked one out and pinned it on the line.

"Spoke to you he did?" he asked.

"He?" Helen opened the door a little to better see her Grandfather's expression. His eyebrows were raised and he wouldn't make eye contact. That wasn't at all like him. "You know what, or who, this is don't you?"

"Uhhh…" Martin slowly turned back to the solution pan. "It's just not easy making sense of these shadows, Pumpkin."

Helen cocked her head sideways and studied his answer. She knew a battle of wits with him would often leave her in second place, *but what to do?*

"I won't use the zoom tomorrow. Perhaps I can get another shot at him if I can get close enough."

Martin paused, removed his glasses, and then looked back at

her. After a deep sigh, he pulled his handkerchief from his pocket and started wiping them. "Perhaps you should give the woods a rest for a while, Pumpkin. You can happen upon the wrong sort there at times—both two-legged and four-legged. That's not to mention that we have the occasional poacher prowling about. I've got a new book on old cameras; I'll lay it out for you. I'm sure you can find something in it to hold your interest for a while."

~ * ~

The next morning, the thought of Martin's old, field glasses tempting her, Helen rose almost as early as Narbie. Easing the bedroom door open, she peeped down the hall. The glasses were still in their place on the back of the door, and her grandmother beyond them in the kitchen. The light aroma of fresh-perked coffee tweaked her curiosity.

"Didn't think you and Grandfather liked coffee, Grandmother," Helen quickly donned her trousers and pullover shirt.

"One of Martin's American friends got him started on the stuff. Actually, it goes pretty well with breakfast."

Helen pulled her hair back in a ponytail, fastened it with a black hair band as she eyed the binoculars. She then noticed her grandmother had the back door open to let a bit of cool air in the kitchen.

"Would you mind if I eat my breakfast on the back porch?" asked Helen. "It's so lovely out there and I wouldn't want to miss an early riser."

"I've already nibbled my way through breakfast, child." Narbie glanced at her. "Your grandfather has already finished his. He's off to pick up a few things at the grocery and the meat market for me. After that, I'm sure he'll make his stop at the Boar's Head Inn, if it's not too early for his daily 'nip'. It'll likely be past noon before he gets back."

Helen slipped on her loafers, picked up her camera, and then walked briskly to the kitchen.

"Tea?" asked her grandmother as she held up a hot kettle from the stove.

"Please. I'm not much on coffee." Helen glanced back at her grandmother, grabbed a sausage, stuffed it into a roll, and then asked, "Would it disappoint you if I took my breakfast to the table on the back porch? I would like to look for that goshawk again."

Slowly shaking her head, Narbie made another and placed it upon a cloth napkin. Laying it on the counter by the teacup in front of Helen, she said, "You're just like your grandfather. You had rather chase after something in the woods than eat or sleep." She then placed a gentle hand on her granddaughter's left forearm. "Don't wander off too far away from the cabin, Helen. You don't know these woods like Martin does and I wouldn't want to have to call for Dempsey's hounds to come and find you."

"Yes, Grandmother."

Helen took the napkin and cup of tea, kissed her grandmother, and then headed for the back door. In doing so, she snagged the strap on the field glasses with one finger. A cool, morning breeze greeted her face as she stepped onto the porch. October had already started turning the leaves and some of them looked as if they were fresh from the painter's palate. Helen sat her breakfast on a little, round table near the steps and then sat down in one of the old, metal chairs beside it.

Where are you now? She raised the binoculars.

The wet grass glistened on the lower end of the yard, taunting the sun's coming. It was peeking through the trees signaling the end of the slight fog that now lay close to the grass near the woods. Helen was about to finish her first roll and sausage when something caused a commotion in the chicken coop about forty paces northwest of the porch.

Hearing her grandmother walking across the wooden floor, Helen turned to see her push the back, screen door open.

"Open the door to the coop, please child," said her grandmother. "That young cock Martin bought the other day is having at my old Rhode Island Red again. Be quick, while he still has feathers."

Helen dropped her roll and sausage to the napkin and ran for the coop. The commotion in it sounded again as she approached the old shed-like building. Dust drifted from the partially open windows and through the planks on the door as Helen slowed just steps from the building. Now, with the sound of things falling to the dirt floor, she could wait no longer.

We don't want to get flogged, Helen, and she reached for the wooden latch. Slowly lifting it, she backed up behind the door and pulled it opened. The chickens came running, flying, and jumping through the doorway and into the open yard. When it looked as if the last one was out, she noticed the huge Red wasn't among them. Martin's young roster was there, but he was so nervous he could hardly be quiet or stand still. Helen eased around the door and peeped inside the dark coop, waving the dust and down away from her face. Then, noticing a ray of light coming from close to the floor on the far right side of the little building, she crept toward it.

"In the way! In the Way!" shouted someone behind her as something brushed past her right leg. The voice sounded both excited and irritated.

Helen screamed and fell against the left wall next to one of the dirty windows. She flung open the window as wide as it would go. With the extra light she could now see the far side of the room clearly. But, what she was now looking at was every bit as puzzling as what she had just heard. The old Red was there all right, but he was wedged, tail first, in the hole where the light had been coming from. She could see the chicken's head and about half of his body.

"Are you coming or going?" quipped Helen as she eased toward the chicken.

Then, with a scraping bump, the rooster left the coop altogether.

"What?"

Helen spun around and ran out of the coop. When she reached the back of the building, she stopped and quickly searched through the woods for some sound or movement. The Rhode Island started fussing again not more that fifteen paces out in the scrub in front of her.

She was about to step in that direction when the same irritated voice from the coop spoke again. "Go back! Go back!" it shouted as the rooster sprang from the scrub and ran past her. "Take the chicken. She's in the woods! You must go back!"

"She?" Helen looked back at her Nikon still setting on the little table with her breakfast. *No time to get the camera,* she thought as she pushed forward through the waist-high weeds.

Just as soon as she started, something burst from the scrub, running away from her.

"Wait," she called to the little red-haired man, but he didn't slow up. "No you don't," she stepped forward, but as she did, she spotted a little, creature lying directly in front of her. "Shoo!" she half-heartedly kicking up the leaves at it, but the furry, football sized thing didn't move a muscle.

She leaned closer, extended one finger, and nudged it.

"A cap?" Helen quickly picked up the garments and waved it at the mysterious fellow. "You've lost your cap!" She ran after him but he was fast on his feet and now a considerable distance ahead of her. *I should be able to catch one so small.*

Racing forward, Helen ran downhill after the little fellow. Low-hanging branches brushed her face, wild berry vines pulled at her trousers. She continued west toward and then past next hill. Finally, her hopes of at least gaining on him had all but vanished. With her heart pounding in her chest and her second breath just a memory, she stopped.

"Geeze! He's just testing my resolve."

She stopped, hands on her knees and gasped for breath as she watched the little fellow from the top of the hill. He had just jumped a five-foot creek like a teenager and was now heading toward an open field.

"How can one three times my age do that?" grumbled Helen. She looked back at the woods behind her. *Is this the third hill?*

Did I turn west after the first or second hill?

Her grandfather had taught her about the importance of a compass, or at least paying attention to landmarks. But the only landmark she had noted when she left the chicken coop was the little figure now disappearing in the field in front of her. Tiptoeing, she checked him once more, but as she did, she lost her footing on something in the grass and fell backwards.

Her world went black with sparkling stars as her head struck something hard in the grass.

"Oh Lord," she groaned as she grabbed her head. A searing pain in the back of her head seemed to explode just behind her eyes. She rolled back and forth until the pain subsided. Eventually, she managed to sit up, and then stand

Grandmother is not going to like this, she thought as she rubbed the egg-sized bump on the back of her head. It seemed as if it had its own heartbeat. She slowly looked back at the creek the little man had just crossed.

"Just great," she groaned, slapping the furry cap against her right thigh. "Grandmother will never let me out of the house again without Grandfather."

But just as she started to guess which way was toward the cottage, she noticed a slow and steady movement about half way down the hill she had just crossed. The gray, furry object moved through the scrub seemed to be following the same trail she had made in the weeds and grass.

Helen knelt in the grass. "A wolf, and a big one at that," she grumbled. Her voice was every bit as weak as she felt. "I can't stay here. It's tracking me. Besides, Grandfather said there were no wolves in England."

Helen moved quickly to the far side of the hill until she was out of sight of the wolf and then started to run east as fast as the scrub and brambles would allow. Ignoring the woodbines and briars pulling at her clothes and tearing at her skin, the fear of such a creature drove her on.

This has to be east, she turned right and faced the edge of the hill she had just left the wolf on. *If that was east, then the cabin is a bit past this and the next hill or so to the south.*

Watching ever so carefully, she ran until she was in sight of the southern edge of the hill she was just on. She paused to check for the wolf. She knew if it saw or heard her, it would hunt by sight, leaving her little or no chance to make it back to her grandparent's cabin.

"There you are," she whispered and watched the huge animal sniff its way up the hill she had just left. *Two hundred yards from me,* she thought, and then spun around to look toward where she believed the cabin was located.

Just as she was about to start again, an elm sapling about thirty paces away and a bit to her right shook violently.

"And there you are again," The little man standing next to it waved for her to come toward him. "Works for me."

Helen ran toward him but by the time she got there, the little fellow was nowhere to be found.

"Ohhh, I've no time for games," she glanced back to check for the wolf.

Checking once again for her newfound friend, she noticed a young spruce in the distance. It was moving the same way the elm sapling had done. She ran, fighting her way through the scrub to the young tree. This time, little fellow was there, picking some kind of small, purplish-black berries from a vine that had entwined itself around the little spruce.

"Step on 'em," he said, pointing to a little pile of what looked to be blueberries in front of her. "Do it quickly now. If the animal sees us, this won't do us much good."

"What are they?" asked Helen as she mashed the berries beneath her feet.

"Berries from a pepper vine." He smiled as he added, "but this might not throw her off."

"Her... Who are you?"

She handed him the moleskin cap she had found.

He brushed his long, red hair back behind his head. "Thanks," he finally said. Quickly taking the hat, he pulled it down firmly in place. His black eyes sparkled at her as his smile widened. "I'm Bumpas," he added, stroking his long red beard, "Billy Bo Bumpas. I guess you can call me Bo." Then, wiping his face with his hands, he began stomping a little pile of his own as he nervously watched for the wolf. "Come, we must go before she sees us. We wouldn't want her to have the advantage."

"She? Her?" Helen sputtered as the little man grabbed her hand, spun her around, and started running.

"Ethrel Ibenus," he said without missing a step.

"Sounds like a poisonous flower, not a wolf," replied Helen, struggling to keep up with the little man.

"Both, I fear," Bo picked up the pace. "She's a long vanquished witch, but she lingered in her dyin' just long enough to cast her spirit in what we now have trackin' us. It's her familiar. Some misguided soul brought her the damned thing from the Canada's when it were no bigger than a badger."

"Familiar? Witches?" Helen asked weakly as she stumbled through the scrub after the little man.

He neither tired nor slowed. The dagger he carried on his belt appeared to be silver and intricately tooled with oak leaves as was its sheath.

"Holy mackerel," she finally said. "You're a dwarf. I don't believe it."

Bo glanced back at her and scowled. "Would you have me

leave you again? We'll see just how fast Old Ibenus brings the be-lievability back to you."

"No, please don't."

Stumbling into the tall grass, Helen ended up on her back, looking up at the little man.

Bo quickly stopped and walked back to where she was sitting. "That's the trouble with most of you human folk. You have to first see to believe."

For the first time, Helen could see he also was beginning to tire. His long, deep breaths slowed as he watched the woods be-hind them.

"I'm tired of running', but don't feel good about facin' her here. This place is much too open. Let's go up the hill a ways. I know of a big, old white oak near its top. Maybe Mrs. Goody-Two-Shoes is close by. I'd hate to be in her debt, but I'd sacrifice that for a little comp'ny right now."

"Who are you speaking of now?" Helen stood and began pulling the grass from her hair.

"I'll tell ya if she comes," he replied as he grabbed her hand again and started up the hill at a brisk clip.

"I see it," said Helen, noting the huge tree up ahead of them. "Its lower limbs nearly touch the ground." Helen checked behind them as they neared the great oak. "Maybe we've lost it."

"That's no 'It' lass," corrected Bo. "That beast she calls Seleene, carries the last remnant of the most evil bein' I've ever come to know. Come. Let's get a little closer to the tree. Her in-fluence will be a bit diluted under this old friend."

The two climbed on top of one of the tree's huge, water bar-rel-sized roots and walked along it to the trunk. Bo then sat down and pulled his dagger from its sheath. Carefully shaving the dark brown bark off, he soon came to the moist, live underwood. Plac-ing his right palm on the bare spot he paused.

"What are you doing?" asked Helen.

"Shhh," hissed the dwarf. "Be quiet, lass, and watch for Ethrel. She is near."

Helen watched down the hill toward the valley, but listened closely as the dwarf spoke a poem to the tree.

"By faith I place my hand on thee

to call the one we cannot see.

For now we are in trouble dread,

from one who has cheated the world of the dead."

He removed his hand, stared at Helen for a moment, and then whispered, "Do you see her?"

"Yes Sir. She's just entered the valley, but she's acting a bit queer."

"Queer?" Bo he scrambled to his feet.

"Yes sir. It's like the wolf wants to track us, but it's having trouble doing it—just like its fighting an invisible foe."

"It's the salt," said the dwarf with a giggle.

"Salt?" Helen looked back at the dwarf. He was bouncing a small, leather pouch in the palm of his right hand. "The wolf will want it, but the witch in him will have to forbid it. Just wondered whose will would be the strongest. We had to have a plan if the pepper berries didn't work." The dwarf then stood and took Helen by the hand. "Lift me up, lass, I would like to see also."

Helen lifted him as best she could until he was sitting upon her shoulders. "Yes, yes," he whispered, shaking both fists in front of him. "If this works, the wolf will have his salt and the witch will be driven out to cross the River Styx, without a coin I pray."

"Is it working?" asked Helen as she struggled to hold the dwarf.

"Let me down. We're not stickin' around to find out." Stepping from her shoulders he added, "Are you rested enough to go again?"

"Guess so, but where? Which way?"

"Come, and follow closely. There's a dwar…game trail at the bottom of this hill. It will take us to within a weak stone's throw of the Professor's place."

"Professor? Do you know—"

"Come, child," interrupted Bo as he wheeled and started running down the hill. "No time for questions. I am guessing we'll have no help from the oak. We must go."

When they came to the trail, Bo paused to catch his breath. He then grabbed a small, oak sapling and began hacking at its base with his dagger.

"What are you doing?" she asked, watching him clean the

smaller limbs from the six-foot staff.

"If she gets past me…" His face grew sullen with worry as he glanced back toward where the wolf was last seen, "and she probably will, you'll need this to fend off the wolf. When she hits this trail, she can track at a run. We'll likely not make it to the cabin." Bo then handed her his salt bag. "If she gets too close, throw a little of this on her and then run like the Devil himself were after you."

The two proceeded to run up the path while Bo continued to clean the staff. Constantly checking the path behind her, Helen gasped, grabbing the back of Bo's jacket.

"Ohhh Bo," she said weakly. "I think I see her."

"That's it." The dwarf shoved the staff into her hands, pulled his dagger, and then pushed Helen behind him. "She'll have to get by me first. You keep runnin' until you see a field on your right. Once there, you'll have a clear view through the woods beyond of the Professor's Cabin."

Before Helen could turn, she saw a blinding flash in the path directly between them and the wolf. "What was that, Bo?"

"Bless my soul!" exclaimed the dwarf as he began to jump up and down. "My prayer's been heard. The old oak didn't fail me."

The sun was now well up to the tops of the trees, making the path and the wolf plainly visible. Only fifty yards separated them now, but the wolf was completely distracted by something and it certainly wasn't salt this time.

"Shhh," hissed Helen. 'Should we hide? She's sure to see us now."

"Matters little now, lass. "We have help, and it comes on the wings of a dragonfly."

"Dragonfly?" Noticing the dwarf was still very much excited, Helen asked, "What's happening? It's looking from one side of the path to the other. Does it not know where we are? Surely Seleene can smell us, maybe see us. Why did it stop?"

"Pure light, yearling. Pure light."

Bo calmed quickly. Slowly dragging his cap from his head, he held it crumpled to his chest. Then, the flash of light came again, and this time it was close to the beast's muzzle.

"Nooo!" screamed Bo, watching the wolf lunge into it.

"There it is again," Helen gripped the back of the dwarf's

jacket.

"Yes, but he didn't get her…He couldn't have got her."

Bo was no longer excited. His tone was laced with fear and a bit of regret.

"Her? Her who?"

Helen's tone was raised, but not with excitement this time. She gripped the back of his jacket. Bo put his hat back on to watch the wolf advance once again.

"It's fool's play to stay here, lass! Run for your grandfather's home!"

Helen, noting the sharp end on the foot of the staff, raised it toward the wolf. Gripping it tightly, she shouted, "I'm not leaving you here with that!"

Bo laughed loudly. "You should've been a dwarf, lass. You're as foolhardy as you are brave."

The wolf, now only fifteen paces from them, lowered his head, raised his hackles, and then started a low, guttural growl. For the first time, Helen got a good look at his eyes. Even at that distance she could tell their orange glow didn't come from any animal she knew.

"Vile creature of darkness!" shouted the dwarf, "You have defiled the beautiful animal that now hosts you, but you'll not have this child! I'll take you to the River Styx myself, and steal the coins on your eyes."

Then, as the beast started snapping its huge, white teeth, there came a wind. It took the leaves and pine needles from the ground and swirled them all about the two, the wolf, and the woods. Shielding her eyes, Helen tried to keep Seleene in sight, but looked upon the form of a young girl instead. All of four feet tall she walked toward them through the wind. Not a long, brown hair on her head was moving. Her green eyes sparkled as she glanced at the dwarf, and then looked at Helen.

Realizing neither of them was going to speak, she said, "Do not run. Do not fear," her voice calm. "I cannot defeat this evil, but I can take it far from here."

She moved with such speed Helen struggled to follow her. The girl's bright green dress quickly became one, long green streak as it circled within the wind and rose above them. Leaves, pine needles, and grass quickly gave body to a huge cyclone as it moved toward the wolf. Bo buried his face inside his hat, but Helen could not look away. Shielding her eyes with her hands from time to time, she tried to keep her attention on the beast.

"Hold to me!" exclaimed Bo as he reached back and tried to steady them both.

With the wolf plainly whimpering, Helen closed her eyes and settled to the grass with the dwarf until the wind subsided.

~ * ~

"Helen," the voice sounded like it came from up the trail a ways. "Helen." This time it was closer, and unmistakable.

"Grandfather!" she exclaimed loudly as she tried to get up, but something was pushing her back down into the grass. "Grandfather!" she screamed as she shut her eyes.

"Wake up, child," came the voice again. "You're scaring us half to death."

Little by little, Helen opened her eyes. The forest was gone and so was the scent of the grass. What she was now lying on was certainly much too soft for the ground.

"Hold still, Helen." Another voice this time. It wasn't Bo, nor her Grandfather.

As a bright light flashed back and forth, the form of a dark-haired, young man slowly came into focus.

"I see no outward sign of a concussion," said the man. He patted her hand and adjusted something wet on her forehead. "Keep a cold compress on her forehead and that bump. Watch those scratches, especially the deep ones. Keep plenty of salve on them," he looked at her Grandmother. "If she gets dizzy, or sick at her stomach, bring her to my home immediately."

"Thanks, Doctor Ray," said Narbie. "When that goose egg goes down, we'll call you again, because I'm going to give her another one."

"Now, now," Martin placed another cool towel on Helen's head. "I'm just glad I found her."

"How did I get here?" asked Helen as she tried to sit up.

"Back down, young lady," Martin gently pushed her back to the pillows on the couch arm. "I found you on a path just southwest of here. You had evidently stumbled and struck the back of your head on a stone in the grass."

Narbie stepped closer and peeped around Martin. "Who is this Bumpas fellow? You were calling for him before you came to."

Helen glanced at the young doctor and then looked back at her grandmother. "I...met someone who helped me when I became lost," she answered, raising her eyebrows to better see how the half-truth was setting in.

"Well," grumbled Narbie as she placed her hands on her hips. "I don't think he helped you at all. You were all alone when Martin found you. I don't know of anyone named Bumpas living around here."

"Neither do I," added the doctor. "What did he look like?"

Helen smiled and slowly sat up, "If I told you what he looked like, and what I think happened to me, the good doctor here would surely put me in the hospital."

"I see," replied the doctor with a slight grin. "A person's imagination is oft times *tweaked* when they're out with a mild concussion. You know, like Dorothy in the *Wizard of Oz*. Just watch her like I said. She should be back in the pink in no time."

Narbie walked Dr. Ray to the door as Helen watched her Grandfather pick up something from the coffee table and place it on the couch beside her.

"You almost lost your hat, Pumpkin. It was lying in the grass by your right hand," he added as he turned to join the two at the front door.

Helen froze with her eyes fixed upon the little, dark brown, and moleskin cap lying next to her. *If the little chicken thief was real, then what of the faerie, and of the wolf...and the witch?*

Part Two
Point of Light

Helen raised her head from her pillow, wiped the sleep from her eyes, and then peered out of her window. The new day was just starting to brighten her grandparent's back yard, coloring the treetops with a bright, golden glow.

Did I dream that someone called my name?

Easing her hand to the back of her head, she gently rubbed the tender spot where the bump was. The thought of her father taking her back to London next month wasn't near as pleasant as it should be. Their home in London had her mother's touch on just about everything but it was a constant reminder that she was gone. With a long sigh, she closed her eyes again and slipped gently away into a half doze.

~ * ~

All too quickly, she woke again. *All right,* she slowly looked about the road she was now standing on.

Much like a wagon trail, it ran in front and behind her but there was not a tire mark anywhere nor did it look familiar. The sun was not very high, adding to the dark and uncomfortable look.

"Come, Helen. I need your help." the familiar voice that woke her spoke again from somewhere close.

Helen slowly looked closer this time. As her eyes adjusted to the low light, her gaze focused on someone standing in the path, only a few paces away wearing the moleskin cap.

"Bo?" she asked just above a whisper, but the dwarf didn't move.

Am I about to face the wolf again?

No sooner had she thought that, than she noticed a dim glow up ahead in the trail. The apple-sized object was about five feet above the trail and drifting soundlessly toward them. Neither slowing nor moving either way, the faint, yellowish glow dodged the dwarf and then shot straight for her face. Helen gasped, but before she could duck, the small sphere brightened to expose the face of a young, brown-haired girl.

"What do you think?" asked the vision. The girl's large, green eyes widened, as she awaited an answer. "Well!" she added loudly.

~ * ~

"Geeze!" exclaimed Helen as she quickly sat up in bed.

She blotted the dampness from her forehead with the sleeve of her nightshirt and looked about the room.

Honeysuckle? she mused. *Is Grandmother into air fresheners now?*

Through her partially opened bedroom door, she saw the kitchen light was on.

"You *are* up," spoke a familiar voice as Grandmother Narbie peeked down the short hallway from the kitchen counter. "I thought so when I saw the little light in your room."

"Light?" asked Helen, watching Narbie tuck her gray hair back under her hair net.

"Yes. I thought it strange for you to use a flashlight and not your table lamp."

Helen looked slowly about the dimly lit room and then replied, "Grandfather's got my flashlight. I've been asleep until just a minute ago. I had a strange dream and…"

Helen's voice trailed off as she got another whiff of honeysuckle, the very same scent she noticed just after the girl in her dream spoke to her.

"Helen, are you all right?" asked Narbie. "You seem distracted by something."

"I'm…fine, Grandmother. I'll be up in a second. Is Grandfather awake yet?"

"He's in the hen house try'n to talk our old hens out of a few eggs. I'm cooking fresh sausage and crumpets, and I've opened a new jar of currant jelly. You'd best hurry. You know how Martin likes that jelly."

"Yes, Grandmother," her words muted by a long yawn.

Easing out from under the sheet and bedspread, Helen shuffled sleepily to the door and shut it. She was just about to reach for the shift-a-robe doors when a light beamed from between them. Snatching her hand back, she stepped back, and then stood staring at the old piece of furniture. Seeing the light fade to dark, she stepped to its left side, slowly opened the left door, and peeped around it.

Quick as a flash, out from the shift-a-robe a green object streaked across the room and hit her pillow so hard it rattled the headboard.

"Ohhh!" exclaimed Helen as she fell back against the wall.

"Are you all right, Helen?" asked Narbie from the kitchen.

"I'm fine, grandmother," she quickly answered, staring at a wee, little girl sitting in the middle of her top pillow. "It was just a big...bug."

"I'm-not-a-bug!" replied the seven-inch girl as she rubbed out a wrinkle in one of her dragonfly-like wings. Dressed completely in green, except for her fawn-colored boots and nearly black moleskin cap, the brown-haired fae looked up at Helen, "You can shut your mouth now. I'm not going to bite you...yet."

"I saw you," Helen finally managed. "You kept the wolf from getting Bo and me, and you were just in my dream."

"Partially right," quipped the tiny girl as she fidgeted with her long brown hair. "I kept Ibenus from getting you. The wolf was just an unwilling participant." Looking up at Helen through the most amazing, orange eyes, she added, "Soooo...what *do* you think?"

"It *was* you," exclaimed Helen, struggling to keep her voice low. "How did you get into my dreams?"

The tiny girl rolled her eyes. "It's just another door. Fortunately, most humans can't see them. I'm Rosebud of Kiendom—the Woodland Faes. Bumpus says you can be trusted. That being said, it means you can learn our ways because he needs your help. He asked for it in what you call a dream. If you agree, I'm to bring you to him."

"Now?" Helen glanced toward her bedroom door, "But what of Grandmother. If she finds me gone, she'll have kittens."

"Ask her again," spoke a timid voice form within the shift-a-robe.

As Helen watched, the door to the large, wardrobe opened slightly. Out from it was tossed one of Helen's heavy, plaid shirts and a pair of denims.

Rosebud slowly shook her head. "You could've at least

brought them to her. After all, it's your mother she'll be helping to save."

"No," the girlish voice spoke again. "Have her answer my father's question first."

The little fae looked back to Helen. "Well? The Professor will handle your absence. We'll see to that."

Helen thought for a moment before she smiled and replied, "In the dream, he asked me for help. I helped him before, and I'll help him again if I can."

The door to the shift-a-robe then moved and out stepped a little, brown-haired girl all of three and a half feet tall. Her brown eyes glistened as she glanced at Helen while picking the pants and shirt from the floor. Trimmed just below her ears, her short auburn hair appeared damp as did her long, brown, flower print dress.

"Thank you. I'm Intwhistle." She held the clothes up for Helen to take. "My mother, Merrymint, was taken by the Hobuerich. They want to trade her for something my father is not eager to give.

"The Hobuerich?" asked Helen. "Who are the Hobuerich?"

"Black faeries—big, pasty-looking faes," answered the woodland faerie. "Bo thinks Ibenus has something to do with it.

"Why me?" asked Helen as she looked at Intwhistle.

Rosebud rolled her eyes to Intwhistle. "Simple," started the fae, looking back at Helen. "Of all the beings the Hobs fear, wizards are right there at the top. But, since there are very, very few wizards left, those who are in their line rank next, especially if they're human."

The little fae took a half step back and bowed. "You are in the line of Alvis. They will see your aura."

Throwing the Woodland Fae an irritated glance, Intwhistle continued. "They will see your aura and respect you more than any of us, she means."

"What about my grandfather?" asked Helen.

Rosebud quickly shook her head. "They're too scared of him. He killed the—"

"Ohhh Rosebud," interrupted Intwhistle. "Let's not go into that right now." The dwarf glanced toward the bedroom door and then produced a clear crystal from her pocket the size and shape of a hen's egg. Holding it tightly with both hands at first, she finally held it out to Helen. "This once belonged to Richard Alvis a long, long time ago in this same land. It was given to one of our people. Broderick Cliffspring was his name. I'll make you a gift of it if you will help us get my mother back."

"And you said your mother's name was?" asked Helen.

"Merrymint Cliffspring Bumpus."

"You're Bo's daughter?" asked Helen.

The little girl nodded, but her smile was weak, not knowing yet if she had made a friend or not.

Helen slowly reached for the stone, but as she did, a dull, yellow light started glimmering within its center.

"What's that?" asked Helen, pulling her hand back.

"Hope!" shouted Rosebud as she shot about the room and then back to the pillow with a thump. "Please take it. It will not harm you."

"Very well," spoke Helen as she reached for the stone. As she took it, the crystal glowed brightly and then faded. "What causes that?"

"A gift," responded Rosebud with a little dance. "It's from one in your line a very long time ago."

Helen shrugged. "I don't have gifts. I'm even having trouble with algebra."

"It's all right." Intwhistle pointed toward the shirt. "Put your clothes on." She snatched the crystal, shoved it into Helen's pants pocket, and then held the clothes up toward her again.

Helen quickly dressed, but upon feeling the stone in her pocked, she paused.

"The shoes! The shoes!" prompted Rosebud. "We may not have much time. The wolf, Seleene, even now searches for something. I feel if she finds what she's looking for, it will be the end of Merrymint."

Helen jerked on her socks and deerskin boots and then stood, looking at Intwhistle. With the dwarf holding her right arm, and the fae pushing at her back, the shift-a-robe quickly opened and she was all but shoved into it.

"Wait! Wait!" complained Helen as she closed her eyes and shielded her face from the clothes and their hangers, but she felt nothing at all.

"How can this be?" she whispered as she looked about the great forest before her. Turning back toward where she had just came, she looked upon a huge oak with a great, yawning hole in its side.

"What are you looking at?" asked Intwhistle.

"Nothing…and everything." Helen turned back around. "The trees are humongous, and the ferns that border the creek behind you have leaves the size of kites." She looked at the side-by-side trail she was standing in. "This looks like the same trail from my dream. How did we get here?"

"Another door," answered Intwhistle as she tugged at Helen's arm. "We're on the Whitestone Trail, close to the southern edge of the Gossamer Swamp. My father's not far from here. We must go right now."

"Fine," agreed Helen with a half-smile. "I couldn't be any more lost."

"Let's go then." Rosebud flew to Helen's shoulder. "If we discuss this any longer, Merrymint is a goner for sure."

Looking both up and down the trail, Helen asked, "Which way are we going?"

"That way," replied the faerie as she flew to Helen's right shoulder and pointed forward. "That's south, kind of. Whitestone Castle, where the Wizard Richard lived used to be behind us a good three days or so. We're coming up to the southern edge of Gossamer Swamp."

"Nobody wants anything to do with this place," explained Intwhistle as they walked on. "Strange things happen here. Folks go in, but don't come out. It's on the edge of the Black Forest—a very strange place also."

"Great." Pulling her shirt more tightly about her, she asked, "Who owns it?"

"Sir Charles Edward Moorhead." Rosebud snickered. "But he died over seven hundred years ago. I guess the Queen owns it now, at least the places I'm willing to go into."

Just after that remark, Intwhistle slowed to a stop, but her gaze held on something up ahead.

"What is it?" whispered Helen as she searched where the dwarf indicated.

"I see it?" responded Rosebud at a whisper.

"What it?" asked Helen.

Intwhistle eased back to Helen's right side and whispered, "Fourth tree on the right. Low limb across the trail."

"Blackbird?" whispered Helen.

"Grackle," corrected the dwarf.

"They've already found us," complained Rosebud as she stomped her foot on Helen's shoulder.

"It's just a bird." Helen's eye roll ended up on Intwhistle. "I've seen flocks of them this time of year where I live."

"You don't see them like Intwhistle," Rosebud explained in a cool tone. "She sees its aura, especially the evil ones. When she was young, Bo noted that. He and Merrymint then changed her name to Intwhistle. The name means she can see things others can't."

"I'll get him. He's just one," decided the faerie.

The little fae streaked from Helen's shoulder, up the trail, and chased the bird up into the huge tree. Almost immediately, Rosebud burst from the tree and raced down the trail straight for them. In less than three heartbeats, the background behind the little fae was flooded with black grackles.

"Run!" shouted Rosebud.

"Get your stone out quickly," exclaimed Intwhistle.

Without thinking, Helen rammed her right hand into her jeans and pulled out the crystal. "It's not even glimmering!"

"Help!" exclaimed Rosebud only a few seconds from them.

"Blow on it!" shouted Intwhistle.

Responding at once, Helen cupped the stone in both hands and blew into them.

First, appeared a yellowish glimmer which quickly turned into a pure, blinding light. It came so quickly and with such intensity, that Helen covered her eyes with her left hand and fell down to her knees.

"Don't turn it loose!" exclaimed Intwhistle. She grabbed Helen's right arm and held it up with the stone still glowing within her hand.

"Incoming!" screamed Rosebud. She streaked toward Intwhistle, lodging herself somewhere upon the dwarf's shirt.

Helen, her eyes still shut, listened for the bird's wings. But instead of getting louder, she lost their sound altogether. Instead, she felt something like dry leaves falling on and all about her head and shoulders. Then, hearing the dwarf laughing, Helen slowly looked up. The ground all around them, as well as up a few paces up the trail, was covered with black feathers. Black down drifted in the air all about them as Intwhistle continued to laugh.

"All right. All right," spoke a muffled little voice right in front of them.

Looking down at a curiously moving pile of feathers, she watched as Rosebud pushed her way to the top.

"Tell her the words, Int," grumbled the little fae. "That rock is about to blind all of us."

"De chrishendo," whispered the dwarf. "Say it."

"De chrishendo," echoed Helen.

The light emanating from the stone faded.

"Quit laughing," snapped Rosebud. Obviously not amused, the little Woodland Fae stood waist deep in the black feathers with her tiny fists on her hips and a scowl upon her face. "So you've found her. You've won the bet."

"Three days?" queried Intwhistle.

"Three-days," grumbled the fae.

"One pound each day?" came another question.

"Yes-yes-yes!" exclaimed the fae.

"What are you two talking about?" Squinting at the little dwarf, she asked, "And what just happened?"

"One just doesn't take it lightly when a bet is won from a faerie," bragged Intwhistle. "You do have at least some of the Wizard Richard Alvis's power, and I just won three pounds of truffles."

Rosebud rolled her eyes. "You just scared the bajeebers out of the Hobuerich. The iridescent buzzards you just destroyed watch for them and the Hobs see what they watch."

"And this?" Helen held out the stone in her right hand.

Rosebud rolled her eyes again and grumbled, "Green as grass juice."

"So was Richard at that age," argued the dwarf and turned to Helen. "That's a wizard's stone. It was used mostly on the head of his staff. You may not be a wizard, but—"

Rosebud broke out in uncontrollable laughter and rolled about in the feathers.

"Come on," suggested Intwhistle, tugging at Helen's right

arm. "She's suffering from a lack of adult supervision. Besides, this is not helping my mother. Put that stone up." She looked back at the fae, her voice stern. "Pull yourself together. We're going to the boat on Gossamer Creek. They might soon be looking for us on this trail. Besides, they won't expect us to pass so close to them."

"But——" started the fae.

"No buts," Intwhistle cut in. "Now go and tell Bo."

Rosebud flew from the feathers. As she approached the tree above them, she left a trail of brightly colored sparks. In an instant, she was transformed into an apple-size ball of light. Helen followed yellow orb through the trees, but lost it as it rose above them and into the sunlight.

On they went, trading the open trail for the scrub, thickets, woods, and the dwarf's sense of direction. Intwhistle, was now content she had found the very one to help save her mother. Helen wondered what it was the dwarf thought she had found.

~ * ~

"Intwhistle?" asked Helen as they came upon a marsh to her left.

The dwarf glanced back. "You're rubbing your arms. Are you cold? I thought it was warm for the first day in October. Is your shirt not heavy enough?"

"I'm fine, but where is this place?"

"We're in the Black Forest at the southern edge of Gossamer Swamp.

Squinting at the little dwarf, Helen asked, "We have a Black Forest here?"

"Well, not much of one right now, but it was more imposing back in Richard's time. We're heading for where it drains. That would be Gossamer Creek. The dwarves keep a small boat hidden there. It will take us to where Rosebud will have my father and his friends waiting."

"I see." Helen stepped up closer to the dwarf. "But what are we going to pass close to?"

"The Hobs," replied the dwarf. Her tone regretful.

"I remember. You spoke of them back in the bedroom. Just how big are they?"

"Your size." Slowing at the edge of a clearing, Intwhistle looked back. "They're a bit thinner and real pasty looking. You won't get a good look at any of them because they all wear long, black robes with hoods, and when they're not walking, they ride hagstorms."

Helen eased up beside the dwarf and looked straight at her "And hagstorms are?"

"Something you need to watch out for. I think they're spelled horses of some kind. Every one of them is as black as night, and unusually fast--even faster than what the elves used to ride. They also dislike outsiders--that being us right now."

Helen looked up at the clearing. "Why are we stopping?"

"Do you remember the grackles?"

Helen nodded.

"There are all kinds of black birds, but those iridescent boogers are possessed." Pointing out across the clearing. "On the other side of this clearing is the creek and our boat. I don't want to be seen. The village of the Hobs is not far downstream from here and so is my father. There's a foot trail on the far side of the creek, but it's in plain sight in many places. The boat will keep us a little below the banks and besides, it looks like a log." She turned to Helen, lowering her voice. "Come quickly. I don't see a thing in the trees or the air."

Grandmother's gon'na have kittens, thought Helen as she ran to keep up with the dwarf.

Just as they drew near the far side, Intwhistle slowed at a blackberry thicket. "This will be a little bit sticky." She added with a bit of a smile, "The Hobs hate the barbs."

"Ohhh my," responded Helen, noting the healthy looking berries. "Are they good to eat?"

"Absolutely, but we haven't much time for that. Follow me and try not to give too much blood. The Hobs' hounds will smell it."

"Hounds?"

Intwhistle remained silent.

"Never mind. I don't even want to know."

As they delicately picked their way through the vines, Helen noticed an elongated little lump in the ground close to the creek's edge. It was covered in grass, but no berry vines.

"You are on an errand for your grandfather," Intwhistle worked her way to the lump. "It will be explained later."

When Intwhistle got to the lump, she bent down and took hold of something in the grass. When she tugged at it, the whole hill moved.

"A blanket?" guessed Helen as the dwarf pulled it aside, exposing an unusual little boat.

Ten feet long and almost three feet wide, the little craft resembled an old log in every detail—complete with attachable limbs stored inside of it.

"Help me with these," requested Intwhistle as she handed Helen half a dozen, three-foot limbs complete with fall-colored leaves. "They'll fit in any of the holes along the sides and edges of this thing."

They hurriedly prepared the little craft and then pushed it halfway into the water. Helen noticed the dwarf had paused at the creek's edge. She was rubbing her arms back and forth.

"What now?" whispered Helen. "Are we in trouble again?"

"It's just me," replied Intwhistle, glancing back with a sheepish grin. "This place drains Gossamer Swamp. Ages ago, when the Wizard Richard Alvis was alive, that place was the home of what they called Water Hags—spelled remnants of a village cursed by an evil wizard." She looked back at Helen. "Come and stand here beside me."

Helen eased around the little boat, stopping at the water's edge.

"Now, feel the water," requested Intwhistle.

Helen paused, glanced at the dwarf, and then looked back at the water. Finally, she knelt and placed her hand lightly upon the surface. Her eyes widened and her lips parted. She quickly removed her hand back and stumbled back onto the grass.

"I don't like this," grumbled Helen, her voice quivered as she wiped her hands on her trousers. "It tingled and made me feel unusually cold." She looked at the dwarf, "I saw…I saw…"

"An ugly, old woman?" guessed Intwhistle.

"How did you know that?"

"I didn't," the dwarf looked down the creek and explained. "Rosebud told me stories about this place. Since then, I've come to know the Professor—your grandfather. He told me of a little girl who had an unusual love of this forest. Until now, I thought only the fae people could do what you just did. You have been on my mind ever since Rosebud told me about your aura." Intwhistle turned and helped Helen stand from the grass. "Rosebud described your blue and violet aura. The blood of Richard Alvis is in you, and that, my dear, is Elfin."

"Awww go on."

"Can you steer a canoe?" asked the dwarf.

"Yes. My father sent me to several Summer camps.

"Good. Help me push this thing into the water and you can sit in the rear." They quickly turned and started tugging at the little craft. Once in the boat, Intwhistle glanced back at Helen. "If what I said was not so, then how did I know what you saw in your mind?"

Helen slowly shook her head as she grabbed a paddle from the floor of the little craft. As she headed the nose of the boat downstream, she replied, "I'm working on an answer for that."

"Work on it lying back these fake limbs," suggested Intwhistle. "There's a rope on the inside of the boat on your right. It has a knot in it to help your grip. Push the knot forward to go left and pull it to go right."

Helen leaned back upon a wide, angled board and listened to the dwarf explain where they were about to go. With her mind already spinning about the vision, the creek, and this person named Richard Alvis, she could hardly pay attention. But she did catch the dwarf saying something about the scenery changing in fifteen minutes, tall, yellow grass, cliffs on the left, and the Hobuerich Village and...

Helen sat up. "Did you say Hobuerich Village?"

"Yes. I spoke of them before we got into the creek. I expect they will be close there somewhere." Intwhistle then pulled two little green balls from her pocket and handed one back to Helen. "Squeeze it and rub the juice on your arms and clothes and lay back down. The Hobs sometimes let the hagstorms in the yellow grass to feed. With this on, they won't smell us."

Helen scraped one with her thumbnail. "Wow!" she said softly. "This stuff is a little piney."

"Cypress balls," explained the Intwhistle. "Now, be as quiet as you can. There's a bend to the left up a ways. When we get out of it, you'll see the yellow grass. Three or four hundred more paces or so and we'll be all but even with the village. But it sits back at least that distance in the grass. The Hobs aren't real active in the daylight. Perhaps we won't see any."

With her head close to one of the leafy limbs, Helen peered out toward the rushes and cattails as they eased by the little craft. But as they drifted closer to the bend, she noticed a shimmering in the corner of her right eye, but when she turned, her vision was fine. Then, there it was again—but again, nothing. Helen rubbed her eyes and that seemed to help. As she steered the boat into the bend, she started to see what Intwhistle had explained earlier. Forty paces or so from the bank on the left, rose a cliff taller than the oaks that grew below it. Looking across the where the creek widened, the tall, yellow grass waved at her in the breeze. In some places it looked to be over her head.

"What's that smell?" whispered Helen. "Smells like old socks."

"Shhh," hissed Intwhistle. "They stink to."

"They?" whispered the dwarf.

"Hagstorms," grumbled Intwhistle. "Now get down and be quiet."

Helen was just about to lower her head when she heard something. It started like a high-pitched horse whinny, but ended up in what only could be described as a low, guttural grunt.

"Shhh," hissed Intwhistle. Glancing back at Helen and whispered. "Stay down and be very quiet or you'll have it in here with us."

It? Helen was too close to whatever 'it' was and far too fearful to ask out loud.

Now, raising up just enough to peek over the edge of the little craft, Helen watched the grass at the water's edge up ahead of them move. Ducking back down, she caught a glimpse of something black step from it. She then heard the dwarf, and her *Ohhh no*, wasn't the least bit comforting. Helen laid still and pushed the little knot slightly away from her. Then, as if things couldn't get any worse, she heard and felt the canoe scrape the rocky bottom, slowing the little craft. Trying to be as quiet as possible, and praying their boat wouldn't stop completely, she watched as a shadow started to pass over Intwhistle. As it got to her legs, every muscle in her body screamed *Look up!* and she did.

"Ohhh my," said Helen weakly as she looked into the red, glowing eyes of the ugliest horse she had ever seen. Thin and willowy, the black mare's unusually long mane hung down the side of its face, touching her legs. White foam oozed from its mouth, down to the underside of its chin, and then drizzled down onto her trousers. With thoughts of jumping out, Helen bolted upright and pushed herself back against the headrest.

Then, with a quick half step backwards, the mare raised her head sharply as her eyes widened. One, high-pitch whiney later and the strange animal bolted from them, leaped upon the bank, and then disappeared into the grass.

"I can't believe it. I can't believe it," Intwhistle exclaimed as she sat up, grabbed her paddle, and began to push the little craft out of the shallows.

Helen, glaring at the grass, then to the slobber on her trousers, and back again, her voice weak. "This isn't right. This is some kind of bad dream." She grabbed the dwarf's right arm. "This is *not* my grandfather's forest. I've never even read about an animal like that. The trees here are huge—some over two hundred feet. That grass is yellowish-green but it's far from dying. The ferns have leaves three feet wide and five feet long, and this stream is five feet deep in places yet I can see every rock on the bottom."

"Shhh," hissed the dwarf. "You're right, partially."

"What part?"

"There aren't many of us dwarves left, even fewer druids, and no full-blooded elves at all. The wizards are all but gone, and the witches are too few to count. Unfortunately, the Hobuerich are still with us here, but your world isn't. It's protected by a powerful charm. If you pay attention, you can almost see those in your world move through here, but only in a glimmer at best. It was a gift by the last Alvis. That huge, old oak you admired just after you walked through your shift-a-robe, is but a doorway to and from your world. The Hobuerich would like to have at it, but they are forbidden. Your world has its own evil. Greed, envy, and false Gods will torment it to the very end.

"But, we're in the same time. Aren't we?"

"Yes."

"Is there another door?" asked Helen.

Suddenly, a white flash streaked from the left bank. Hearing something strike the left side of the boat, Intwhistle quickly reached and grabbed the line attached to an arrow embedded there. With the morning sun streaming through the trees above them on the cliffs, she held on. A dwarf quickly stepped from the rushes and cattails and began pulling them toward the left bank.

"Long Barr," whispered Intwhistle.

"Stay in the boat," he whispered back.

Helen sat up to see a stout-looking dwarf well over four feet tall, pulling on the line. Looking in his fifties, his long gray hair was pulled to the back of his head and tied with a piece of red twine. His bushy beard and mustache completely surrounded his big, bulbous nose.

"Glad to see you found her," he whispered. His blue eyes sparkled as he looked at Helen. Your father and the others are down the creek a little ways."

Helen felt a little more at ease, but the strung bow on his shoulders and the hatchet in his belt worried her nonetheless. "Have you found Intwhistle's mother?"

The dwarf faced her and half bowed. "Thank you for your concern. The Hobs have her in the cave where they enter their caverns," he glanced back at Intwhistle. "The cave has a vent at the top. We'll use it to surprise the watch. Now hold on while I pull you through these rushes and on to the bank." He looked at Intwhistle again. "Did you win your little bet with the fae?"

"Yes," Intwhistle's smile broadened. "That and then some. Helen even bested a flock of grackles and fended off a hagstorm just up the creek a little ways. The Hob horse had us cold but must have seen her aura."

"Really," responded Long Barr weakly, his gaze narrowing on the young human. "I hope that spooked hagstorm doesn't tip off the Hobs."

"Don't go supposin'," spoke a little voice from just above them.

Looking up, Helen spotted Rosebud atop a bent down cattail.

The little fae continued. "She does have an impressive aura, but as for the craft, I can only guess."

As the boat nosed into the bank, Long Barr beckoned to them. "Get out quickly. The day is not going to wait for us. The others are planning what to do as we speak and Bo will want to start as close to noon as possible. Remember, the black faes sleep during the daylight hours, but always leave a watch."

For a good thirty minutes, Helen, Intwhistle, and Rosebud followed Long Barr along the banks with the cattails and rushes between them and the creek. Helen, peeked through the plants from time to time and could only see the tall, yellow grass on the far side. However, as Long Barr slowed, she noticed a thin line of light gray smoke well beyond the creek and out into the yellow grass.

"That's where the Hobs are holding my mother," whispered Intwhistle. "My father must be around here close."

As they continued south, Helen noticed a group of dwarves in the distance. They were sitting around four or five coarsely woven, brown sacks, obviously eating breakfast.

"Geeze," whispered Helen as her empty stomach grumbled.

Bo, seeing the approaching group first, stopped eating and quickly stood. He placed his left index finger across his lips. Holding up his food bag, he beckoned for the group to join them.

"I hope that's food," whispered Helen as Long Barr picked up the pace.

As they approached Bo warned, "There's a small group of Hobs out of the cave. Seems like one of their mounts panicked and routed them." He then looked past Long Barr to his daughter. "Who won?"

Intwhistle glanced at Rosebud on her right shoulder and then raised her eyebrows.

"She did, and the halfling used the stone on the grackles." grumbled the fae, much to the dwarves amusement.

Watching the dwarves closely, Helen noticed one long-bearded, red-headed fellow stop chewing as if frozen. Slowly standing, his penetrating, ice blue eyes stared at the human child before them. He looked well into his sixties.

"I am Borack Cliffspring—son of Broderick," he finally stated most reverently. "The stone you used to destroy the birds was passed down through three generations to finally get to, and be used by, another Alvis. What is your name, child?"

"Helen Martin, Sir,"

The dwarves, every one of them, stopped eating and stood silently, looking at her. Finally, one younger, beardless fellow stepped forward with one of the bags. He pulled out a small, round loaf of yellow, thick-crusted bread and two oblong sausages and offered them to Helen. The four-foot man's green eyes sparkled as Helen reached for them.

"I'm Perryman Elfwyck," he managed and forced a smile. "We have little money here, but please accept this toward what we will owe you for your help in getting our Merrymint back."

Helen glanced at Bo, not quite knowing just what to say. She finally replied. "I'm not here to be paid, Perry. Bo and Rosebud saved me from Seleene not long ago. If it wasn't for them, she would have killed me. I owe them a life debt." She glanced at Rosebud. "I don't understand what frightened the ugly horse, or what happened with the crystal. I just hope I don't fail you all."

"Well spoken," responded Borack.

"Effort is all that's required, child. You have come to us and that is already done." Bo then looked at his daughter. "Merrymint is within the cave that shelters the Entrance to their caverns. We will try to get her out through the vent hole at the top of it."

"There's just so few of us, father," tears began to track their way down Intwhistle's cheeks. "What if they are alarmed? What then? We'll never get her out passed the Hobbs."

"What?" Rosebud grabbed the right side of the little dwarf's shirt collar. "I can't believe my ears—a dwarf giving up?" She swung around and looked into Intwhistle's eyes. "Not to worry. I've already taken care of the problem." She turned her attention to Helen.

"Don't look at me," replied Helen, holding up both hands. "I haven't figured out how I got away from the wolf the last time I was with Bo."

With pursed lips and squinted eyes, Rosebud stomped her foot. "*Nobody* has an aura like *yours* without some kind of talent. Work on it!"

"Enough talk," interrupted Bo. "Eat quickly. We leave when our scout returns and only if his report is favorable."

Helen took a seat in the grass with the others and began pulling apart the crusty, yellow bread. The bits of orange cheese and the aroma of yeast spurred her appetite for the strange looking sausages. *Fresh pork, sage, and chives,* she thought at her first nibble through the tender casing. Watching the dwarves closely, she began to realize once more that this was no picnic for them or her either. Their bows were strung, quivers full, and the edges on their black hatchets looked like polished chrome.

Then, with her mouth full of sausage and bread, she heard someone speak behind her.

"Britt chld," it said in a low, guttural voice. The words were strange, and incomplete somehow.

"What?" Helen quickly turned and looked at Long Barr, and then at Intwhistle.

Raised eyebrows were her only answer, for their mouths were also full of food.

"Never mind," Helen glanced behind the two but there was no one else there.

As she took another bite of sausage the strange voice spoke to her again.

"Furries gwen aunder. Harskin weknd," it spoke in the same confusing way.

Helen wheeled quickly, looked at Long Bar and Intwhistle, and then all about the huge, old white oak they were under, but there was no sign of anyone except Rosebud on a limb just above them. Her faced was buried into one of the bread pieces.

Intwhistle quickly leaned closer to her. "Are you all right? You look as if you're looking for something."

"Someone," corrected Helen. "Didn't you hear it? Someone spoke to me two times. The last time it seemed to come from this big oak we're under."

Rosebud stopped munching on her cheesy bred and looked up into the leaves above her. "That's it," she said weakly. Dropping the bread, she quickly flew to Intwhistle's right shoulder, looked back up into the tree, and then grumbled, "I had a feeling I wasn't alone up there."

"It's just the breeze rustling the leaves," quipped Intwhistle. "The wind's got up ever since we left the boat."

"What did it sound like?" asked Rosebud.

"Words of some kind, but I couldn't really understand them. Sounded like 'brit child and 'furries gwen under' and then it said, 'Harskin wekend'."

Barack's eyes grew wide as the bit of bread and sausage he

held in his hands fell to the grass. Slowly standing, he looked up into the limbs of the old oak behind Helen and the others.

"I don't really believe what my old ears are hearin'," he finally got out. "Could it really be possible?" He looked down at Helen and smiled. "Ever talk to trees, young one?"

"Trees?" echoed Helen, squinting. "No. Not really."

"I believe you did hear someone," stated Borack. "That bein' is an Int; that is to say, the spirit of a Druid that has went 'into' a tree. Faes call them Oak Men or Green Men. They move through the roots of the oak, the ash, and the willows. Some believe the Romans and Saxons didn't kill all the Druids before those interlopers left the Isles. The legend that lingered, tells us they 'melted' into the woods." He then smiled at Helen. "You can define 'melted' any way you want. Back then, they used the term 'Live Oaks'. I think they were referrin' to the oaks that contained those spirits. The Hamadryads, or oak faes, move with, tend to, and protect the tree the spirit has entered into." Borack turned to the other dwarves. "She mentioned Furries. That's an old word meanin' evil faes. I think it now to mean the Hobs. The 'Whoever' that spoke to Helen told her they had gone back to the caverns. The 'Whoever" also called her a 'Bright Child'. That assumption I am now beginning to believe. That being said, I can only believe the third thing it said to Helen. That is that Harskin Truft has fallen to some kind of injury."

Looking down at Helen, Bo stepped forward. "Did anyone mention the scout's name where this child could hear it before now?"

Everyone slowly shook their heads.

"Done then," Bo continued to look at her. "Lass, I think you have just discovered your talent, or at least one of them. You can talk to, and have evidently found favor with an Int."

"A what?" Helen squinted at Bo.

"An Int, yearling. They are, some think, all that is left of the true Druids. As the Celtic legend goes, the few that were left, took to the oaks to escape the Romans.

Although they wanted to rejoice, the other dwarves chose to jump and dance silently in a weird and triumphant celebration.

"Shhh!" hissed Borack. "We'll see the Hobbs soon enough. We don't need to see 'em right now."

"We go now," Bo looked at Rosebud. "Sweet, little girl, do you think you can check the way before us over the tall grass without bein' seen?"

"I will, Bo, but I don't think the Hobs will be too active."

"And why not?"

Helen looked to see a young dwarf of forty years or so step up beside Bo with his eyes squinted at Rosebud. His short, black beard cut close to his face made it look rounder than most, and his black eyes held an irritated look of distrust.

Looking at Helen, he quickly removed his hat. "Pardon me, My Lady. I am called Fairweather. I must address this if you please."

"Very well," replied Helen.

Quickly looking back at Rosebud, he snapped, "I caught it when you said you had 'fixed it'. I didn't think you were talkin' about our Bright Helen. Just what is the 'It' you fixed?"

"Uhhh…" The little fae paused, looking back and forth between Intwhistle and Bo.

Fairweather stomped his right foot. "I can't hear you, you little, mischievous point of light. Fess up! What did you already do?"

Rosebud's countenance changed from mildly passive to a darkened thunder cloud. She glared at the presumptuous dwarf. "I saved your bacon, you sawed off human. I don't care if you are related to Bo, I'll call the hornets on you if you disrespect me again."

"Just calm down a little." Holding out his hands between the two, he looked at Rosebud. "We really need to know what you did."

"Not much, really. I was looking for truffles for 'Little Miss Lucky' over there when I spotted a huge foxglove plant. Gathering a few leaves, I flew as fast as I could to the caverns of the Hobs. One of the Hobs, the one that was supposed to be watching Merrymint, was wheeling out feed for those tainted horses they ride. When he had his back turned, I hid under the bed of the one-wheeler and he took me right down into the cavern and into their huge kitchen. It was so hot and humid I could hardly stand it. They were cooking a gigantic pot of some kind of smelly soup," she looked at Intwhistle. "That's when I tore the leaves up in tiny bits and threw them into the mix."

"That's a dangerous sedative," stated Borack with raised eyebrows. "Too much and they'll be seein' things, throwin' up their toenails, or worse. How much did you put in?"

"It was a big pot. I had four young leaves on a string, let them stay in the boiling soup for about ten minutes, and then took them out. They were pouring it up when I left." Smiling, she added, "It won't kill them, but it will slow them down a little. You can thank me later."

Bo glanced at Borack. "We need to go now. By the time we make it through the yellow grass, they will have had at Rosebud's stew." He nodded at the little fae. "Check for us now if you please, My Lady."

"Done," replied Rosebud with a smile. Rising from Intwhistle's shoulder, and in a puff of sparkling blue, yellow, and green dust, she changed into a dull, yellow point of light the size of a small apple.

"Well I never," replied Helen weakly as she watched it drift up, through the tree limbs, and into the sun above them. "Where is she?" Helen looked all about and above the trees.

Smiling at Helen, Intwhistle said, "And you won't see her. She *is* the sunlight now."

"We'll cross here." Pointing toward the stream, Borack added, "It's up to Helen's waist, so all the rest of you might best get your possibles up to your shoulders or higher. It's gon'na be a cool evenin'."

Bo turned to Helen. "Take this. You might need it if things go badly."

Looking down to the dwarf's outstretched hand, Helen noted a twelve-inch dagger with gilded handle and etched blade.

Ohhh, Grandma's surely gon'na give me another bump.

"Thanks," she said weakly, and took the dagger.

Wrapping it in a handkerchief provided by Fairweather, Helen watched the dwarves tuck their weapons, food, shoes, pants, and other things into their bedrolls and hoist them to their shoulders. Noticing their silent laughter, she tried not to look at their brightly colored boxers.

"Come, girls," quipped Borack, "Let's get a little wet."

Helen looked down at Intwhistle and whispered, "If Grandmother knew about what we are now doing, Grandpa and I would have to spend the rest of the month in the chicken coop."

"There are always confrontations. There are but a few of us left in the world—three colonies of dwarves and one of the Hobuerich Clan. I'm at a loss for words at the Int you have just heard."

Long Barr placed his hand on Intwhistle's left shoulder. "Come, girls, we go now. Whatever happens, you just stay close to me. Understand?"

The two girls nodded, looked at each other, and then reluctantly followed the dwarf toward the cattails and rushes.

Helen, quickly removing her shoes, looked down at Intwhistle. "Let me help you. The water is not as deep for me."

"Thanks," replied the little dwarf as she reached up for her new friend.

"Wow," shivered Helen. "Cold is an understatement." She eased closer to Long Barr and whispered. "Why did the Hobs kidnap Intwhistle's mother?"

The dwarf looked back and smiled at Helen's attempt to help Intwhistle. "It's always the way with them when they want something. There are only two portals left into your world from where we are protected—one above ground, one below, and both neatly hidden. Only dwarves, and those allowed, can use them. Allowing the Hobuerich access to your world would be unthinkable. Your world is already full of men. They are all too easily corrupted from the evil that already exists there. The times of the elves and wizards are over and the balance between good and evil is now left to us alone, with the help of those who watch."

So...they're after one of the portals, mused Helen.

She tapped Long Barr on the back. "But what about Ibenus? How is she getting through?"

The dwarf slowly shook his head as he waded with the others and approached the far bank. "Some time ago, she captured a young dwarf named Reuben. We never saw him again. I believe, somehow, that he told her about Fiscar's Pond." He grinned, "don't believe she knows about the shift-a-robe 'cause you haven't seen her in your home."

"That name you referred to with the pond sounds familiar."

The trim, gray-haired dwarf glanced back, but said not a word as they stepped out of the water and onto the bank.

"Here," he helped Intwhistle from Helen's arms. "We need to be really quiet as we enter the grass. Don't want to have to deal with the hagstorms or the hounds."

Then, as they pushed well into the tall grass, Bo stopped and looked back at the others. "I don't like this," he whispered and looked back at Borack. "You think we're headin' in the right direction? If so, how close are we?"

"Striton ta clerin," the same, strange voice spoke within Helen's mind.

Helen grabbed Long Barr's arm and lowered her gaze, listening for more words.

"Wait a minute," Borack frowned as Helen held her head. "Young one, did you hear the Int again?"

Helen nodded. "Are there any trees in this grass?"

"A few. Oaks only," replied Long Barr.

"Again, I didn't understand it. Sounded like, 'Strit on ta clern'." Still holding her head, she added, "I don't like this. Why is it I am the only one who can hear him?"

"He obviously likes you, Helen. He just told you, or us, to go straight on to the clearing." Bo placed his hand on her shoulder and squeezed. "We don't fully understand the craft, young one. Why don't you ask his name the next time he speaks?"

"But where is he?" asked Helen.

"Almost everywhere," replied a young dwarf. A big smile worked its way through his gray mustache under a big, bulbous, pink nose. "He's in the roots below the grass and some of the trees above it. I'm Dullbriar," he announced as he slowly extended his hand toward her.

"He's one of our archers," explained Bo.

"Glad to meet you, Sir," replied Helen, shaking his hand.

"As are we all to meet you, Halfling. They favor the Oaks mostly and…" Dullbriar's voice trailed off as he quickly turned and reached for his bow. "Which way," he whispered as the other dwarves quickly reached for their weapons.

Helen looked at Intwhistle.

"Something's coming this way in the grass," she replied.

"Wait! Wait!" Rosebud shouted as she flew up and clung to the right shoulder of Helen's jacket. Spinning around, she pointed a shaky finger right where they were looking. "Merrymint is coming and she's helping Harskin. He's been stabbed in the right thigh by one of those pasty devils."

"Great, dear lady. You've solved two of our problems already. Looks like your fox glove remedy is working for us," Bo exclaimed as he looked back at Borack. "Just as soon as we have them two, we'll go quickly from here. We don't want to be tied to what's happenin' in their caves right now."

"Agreed," replied Borack.

As they all watched through the yellow grass, Helen edged closer to Bo. "Do you think the plant Rosebud used might have killed any of them?"

Bo glanced past her face to the one sitting upon her right shoulder.

Rosebud pursed her lips, raised her eyebrows, and then quickly shook her head. "Uhhh," she replied as she flew up from Helen's shoulder and above the grass only to return quickly. "Merrymint and the scout are here and company's not far behind. I think they might've seen me leave."

"What?" snapped Fairweather, looking up at the little fae.

Rosebud rolled her eyes. "All right. All Right. They did see me leave, but at least they didn't hit me with those big frying pans."

"Anythin' else you failed to tell us?" grumbled Fairweather.

Stepping between the two again, Bo snapped, "Enough talk. We've got to get out of this grass and make it to the other side of the creek right now."

Then, as Merrymint and Harskin pushed through and joined them, Borack put a shoulder under the scout's right arm. "Got'ta go, young dwarf. Evil's right behind you two.

"At least I'm not bleedin'," said Harskin.

"Good!" Dullbriar jerked his axe from his belt. "I already hear them darned elk hounds, and they sound too close for comfort."

"I hear them too." Perryman Elfwyck tried to peer back through the grass. "I'll bet my pointed ears they've turned 'em loose on us."

Hearing that, Bo quickly put his right shoulder under Harskin's left arm. He and Borack ran him through the grass.

"Elk hounds?" asked Helen, holding tightly to Intwhistle's

left hand.

"They're huge, brown and black, and mean-looking, bearded hounds almost as big as our Shetland ponies. The Hobs train them to kill whatever they're sent after." The little dwarf looked right at Helen. "That being us right now."

As the howling of the tracking hounds grew louder, the little group burst from the grass so fast half of the dwarves ran off the creek's bank and into the water.

"Don't stop now!" yelled Long Barr. "Keep goin' to just under that same, old oak. We'll take 'em when this creek slows 'em down." He picked up Intwhistle, helped Helen into the water, and then yelled. "Fairweather! Bitterthorn! Dullbriar! Join me on the far side with arrows to string!"

Silently, the three dwarves scrambled upon the far bank and readied their bows. Long Barr, helping the girls onto the bank, motioned for them to get under the old tree and away from his archers.

"Helennn," spoke the Int once more. The voice was so loud she fell to her knees and grabbed her ears. "Bring the dwarves to meee," added the Int.

"Who are you and where are you?" Helen screamed.

"I-am-Limbisconn! You are facing me, child. Have the dwarves shield themselves. Harm not the animals. I will discourage them and the Hobuerich."

"What do you hear!" exclaimed Borack. He roughly pulled Helen from the ground, causing Rosebud to flee to the oak limbs above her.

"Careful with this child!" shouted Long Barr as he grabbed the older dwarf's arm.

Quickly yielding to the younger dwarf, Borack faced Helen. "We need to know now, halfling. Please tell us."

"The Int is here," explained Helen. "Do not harm the hounds."

"Here?" questioned Borack.

"There!" shouted Helen. "He's in this old oak."

Rosebud flew from the oak and back to Helen's right shoulder. "I knew it! I just knew it!" exclaimed the little fae.

"We're not to protect ourselves?" asked Dullbriar.

"Should we just kneel and bare our throats?" asked Borack.

"Follow me," Helen trotted toward the trunk of the old tree.

"Do it!" Bitterthorn pointed toward the old oak and added, "She hears the Int!"

"I'd climb it if I could get a grip," shouted Borack.

He and the others gathered around Helen, now sitting on one of the old tree's bark-covered roots. As the howling grew louder, thirteen souls huddled close to one halfling, and wondered what was going to happen next.

Borack, obviously overshadowed by doubts once more, placed a hand upon Helen's right forearm. "You heard it, right?"

Helen nodded. "Just as clear as I just heard you. And I'm still just as scared."

Glancing toward the grass, Long Barr glanced at Dullbriar and asked, "How many hounds?"

"A dozen or more," he sheathed his arrow, put his bow over his shoulder, and then joined them.

"Ohhh my," groaned Helen weakly as the first hound broke from the grass.

Its fur was wavy, and a dirty, black and brown blotched color. Over three feet tall and with hair hanging ten inches from the bottom of its jowls, the beast stared at them.

"It's a bit jaded," whispered Long Barr. "Watch its ears turn toward the grass. It's listenin' for the others to join him."

"Then, we're in for it," added Borack.

"It fears the water," guessed Dullbriar, gesturing toward the creek. "Somethin's in the water."

Intwhistle looked up into the limbs and leaves of the old oak and pleaded. "Please don't let our faith in Helen be diminished by such an evil as this."

"So much for the water," Bo raised his voice as they watched other hounds join the first and then pile off into the water.

Then, as the hounds swam toward them, there came a voice so much like thunder, it rattled their chests. "Bow your heads with the Halfling, little dwarves."

"I heard it!" shouted Intwhistle as tears rolled from her cheeks.

"As did I," added Bo.

Needing no further convincing, they all bowed their heads as the elk hounds swam toward them. When they jumped onto the bank, it seemed as if every other leaf upon the old oak began to fall and become alive. Flying through the air in a clockwise motion, a living, green wall formed around the outer reaches of the old tree. As oak leaves fluttered by her ears, Helen tried to shelter Intwhistle, but the temptation was too great for the halfling. She raised her head and watched the happening. The top of the green wall quickly rose to twelve feet above the ground. Its rustling sound easily drowned out the hounds and approaching Hobuerich.

Intwhistle slowly raised up, but remained very still. "Listen. The hounds are yelping."

"They're scared," replied Bitterthorn without looking up.

Gradually raising his head, Bo said, "The Hobs are also. I can hear them fighting and cursing something."

Dullbriar stood, his fists raised triumphantly, and shouted, "They're fighting the Dryads. They're cursing at the oak faeries."

"The Dryads still live also!" shouted Bitterthorn.

Without hesitation, the young dwarf, Bitterthorn, stood and cheered on those who he knew, but could not see. As the sound of the hounds and Hobs faded, the others slowly stood to join Bitterthorn—shouting, dancing, and some even crying. Little by little, they watched as the sound and intensity of the rustling leaves eased. One by one, each after the other, they drifted up and back into the old oak. Some even drifted close to, and passed between the celebrating dwarves. One in particular, paused to float between Intwhistle and Helen.

"Gracious," said Helen weakly as she stared at not a leaf, but a being she had never seen before.

Dressed in tattered shades of green and brown, the twelve-inch girl appeared to be sixteen or so, as the world of men judge age. However, there was nothing childish about the fae. Her brown hair looked as if it was combed by a pine cone, but in her big, hazel eyes, there was a kindness her smile was quick to mimic.

Flittering closer to Helen, she said, "Bright Child, I can see the good in you. The Old One was right. The *Creator* did favor you."

The Dryad smiled warmly at her and then flew back into the oak so quickly she seemed to disappear. Although the others tried to follow the fae, their efforts left them searching among the limbs and leaves of the old tree.

"Geeeze," exclaimed Rosebud as she stepped from behind Helen's collar. "That tree has more life in it than a mosquito pond. I'm truly surprised they are still here."

"They have done their job well in protecting the Int."

Bo turned to Helen. "Did he, by any chance, give you his name?"

The other dwarves quickly stopped talking and turned toward Helen.

Helen nodded. "Should I tell it?"

"Good question." Borack smiled at her integrity. "Your answer is a resounding yes, but only to us, or perhaps the Professor."

"Very well. He said his name is Limbisconn."

Bo scratched his head, but the others remained quiet. Then, as a smile graced his face, he replied. "The name indicates a green wizard, but it rings no bells with me."

"Well, we got a good deal more than we came for. Now, I suggest we get these ladies away from here and back to their homes before the Hobs work off what they've just been through." Bo glanced back at Long Barr. "You said the Witch was searchin' for somethin'. Do you know what it is and where she is lookin'?" he added as the group started moving north, along the east side of the creek.

Long Barr scratched the back of his neck and looked down at the path. He finally replied, "When I was a young dwarf, I became a friend of a young, halfling girl. She was a healer. Unfortunately, she had an adopted sister who could be very wicked at times. When my friend challenged her for one of her evil deeds, the wicked one spelled her—imprisoning her within a tree." Long Barr shot a look at Borack before he continued. "I believe the halfling's staff is what Ibenus seeks, but she doesn't know how to get at it."

Slowing, Borack looked back at Long Barr, "And the Evil, adopted one is…"

"Ibenus," answered Long Barr, passing the dwarf.

"Perhaps she will seek the girl also, now that we have Merrymint," said Rosebud.

"Quite possible," agreed Bo and shrugged at Long Barr. "Do

you know where this tree is?"

Long Barr slowly nodded. "It is several miles south of where the Professor is living now, and not far from here. But remember, the witch knows of Fiscar's Pond and she could be near the Professor's cabin also."

Borack stopped and took hold of Bo's shoulder, his voice stern. "Wait just a minute. Haven't we had enough of this wicked, old bat? All we have to do is kill one, flea-bitten wolf." He then paused, watching the others closely but when no one responded he continued. "Fiscar's Pond is our answer. Don't you all see? The trail to Old Fiscar's shack is just up ahead a ways. We can set a trap for Seleene, kill her, and our troubles will be over."

"Perhaps you're right," agreed Long Barr and he turned to face the others. "I know my archers would greet a chance to eliminate this threat."

Bo turned to Borack. "Perhaps you should take Helen, Intwhistle, and Merrymint to their homes. I will take Long Barr and his three bowmen with me to Old Fiscar's shack."

Intwhistle moved from Merrymint's side to face her father. "Please don't seek the wolf, Father. Even in Seleene, she could still be very dangerous."

Bo smiled at his daughter and stroked her short, brown hair. "That's why you, your mother, and Helen aren't going. Ibenus's threats and demands were, and have always been horrible. Through the Professor, we got a little relief, but we simply cannot allow her back in human form." He gestured toward Helen. "Tell the Professor what we're about to do. I think circumstance has carried where the staff is hidden to his world also." Bo looked down at his daughter. "Go tend to your mother. I and the other dwarves will be just fine."

With a half-step back, Intwhistle's eyes quickly filled with tears. Then, with her voice quivering, she spoke. "Father, I fear I will not see you ever again."

"It's just a mean old wolf, my dear. We will be fine."

Although she spoke not another word, Intwhistle struggled to keep her composure. Her cheeks remained moist. A short time later, as they approached a badly grown over footpath, she could stand it no longer.

"Father," she pleaded as she trotted up to his side. "Let Helen and I come with you. You've seen what happened with the elk hounds. Maybe she and this Limbisconn can protect you again."

"No Pumpkin. I think not," Bo stopped and then knelt to look into her eyes. "I'm not sure the Int would approve of what needs be done. Besides, we'll do our own killin'. This is a personal thing."

Watching her father stand, the younger dwarf backed away slowly. With her voice still quivering, she replied, "Yes, Sir," and then waited for her mother to catch up.

In barely half an hour, the little group stopped at a rocky ford where a little stream on the far side joined Gossamer Creek.

Helen watched silently as Bo hugged and kissed Merrymint. Smiling down at Intwhistle, he added, "No tears, Pumpkin," his voice gentle. "Let me see a smile."

"I'm scared for you and the others, Father. She's still a powerful, old Hag."

Bo stooped down, hugged her, and then gently pushed her back to arm's length. "She's a bodiless spirit, seekin' shelter in a dumb animal. I have not a thing against Seleene, but if it means going through her to get to Ibenus, then so be it. Now, stay with your mother and let us finish this thing."

Intwhistle, very quiet now, eased closer to Merrymint and then watched as Billy Bo Bumpus, Fairweather, Bitterthorn, Dullbriar, and Long Barr filled their food sacks from what Borack and the others had left in theirs. As those five crossed the stones in the rocky ford, Intwhistle eased close, and then took Helen's hand but said nothing.

It wasn't long before Bo and the others disappeared in the overgrown grass of the footpath that would lead them to Fiscar's shack and the pond.

"We must go now," whispered Borack to Merrymint. "Long Barr and his archers will protect Bo.

Talk was sparse at best as the little group continued north toward the Whitestone Trail. Helen watched as the little dwarf released her hand and moved to her mother's side. But soft words, hugs, and back rubs did little to dry her moist cheeks.

Once on the Whitestone Trail, it took less than an hour to get to the old, hollow oak—the 'door' to Helen's room.

Borack slowed, and then stopped the little group. Looking

back at Intwhistle he said, "Show her how it's done, Little One."

"We're here, aren't we?" asked Helen, noting the old tree just a weak stone's throw from them. She turned to Intwhistle. "Fiscar's Pond is the second door?"

Intwhistle nodded.

"Grandfather Martin knows Edmond Fiscar," explained Helen.

He's referred to him as the 'Little Fellow' several times. Is he…"

"A dwarf," interrupted Borack. He pointed to a woven, brown basket in front of the tree. "Your Grandfather, the Professor, has told Mrs. Narbie he sent you to fetch sweet potatoes from Merrymint. There they are in the basket. However, you are responsible for the extra time this little adventure took. Be inventive, but try not to lie."

"I will," replied Helen.

She and Intwhistle walked toward the hollow tree. Upon arriving there, Helen glanced at the basket and then turned to Intwhistle. "Would it help if you stayed over with me for a little while?"

"I would like that very much, but not just now. I must get back with my mother and await my father's return. Now, you know that the tree in front of you is a portal from your world to ours. Keep it secret. Just walk into the darkness and reach your hands out for the inside of the shift-a-robe door."

Helen looked back at Borack. The dwarf slowly pulled his hat from his head, and bowed. She then picked up the basket, smiled back at Intwhistle, and then stepped into the darkness. The smooth wood of the door was there.

Part 3
Revenge of the Black Witch

Still aware of what just happened, and the vindictiveness of the Hobuerichs, Bo pushed through the eight-foot hog weeds and Johnson grass like a hunter. Although the noonday sun was far from hot, he was sweating nonetheless.

"How far is the cabin?" asked Bitterthorn as he stroked his neatly trimmed, black beard and mustache repeatedly.

"About twenty more minutes." Bo wiped the moisture from his face with his shirtsleeve. "The pond is a weak arrow shot from there."

He glanced back at Bitterthorn and smiled. The young dwarf now seemed to be preoccupied with the condition of his long, black hair. Tightening the leather band just wasn't, apparently, working for his long pony tail.

"Get your mind off your hair, young one," grumbled Bo. "It's Seleene you should be worried about now."

"The devil take the wolf!" Bitterthorn pulled his bow from his shoulder. "Is Old Fiscar still alive?" Not getting an answer, he looked out through the weeds, and then back down to the trail. "There's been someone here." He stooped down to inspect what looked to be the tracks of a horse.

"Sufferin' spinach!" complained Fairweather, all but falling over the young dwarf. He straightened his hunting cap and repositioned his satchel. "If you're not slappin' me with those tall weeds, you're stoppin' to check somethin' in the path."

"We have tracks," said Bitterthorn, looking up at the frustrated, old dwarf.

"What?" asked Fairweather, cupping his hand behind his right ear.

"Never mind," grumbled Bitterthorn.

Bo stopped and looked back at Bitterthorn, now also examining the path. "What did you find?"

"Not a thing," answered Bitterthorn.

Dullbriar rolled his eyes and replied, "Can I shoot the kid now, Bo. You said I could if I couldn't teach him anythin'."

"Not just yet," quipped Bo as he looked over Fairweather's shoulder.

"It's a horse." Holding out his hand toward the curious set of tracks, Bitterthorn added, "Got one rider goin' and commin'."

Looking at Bitterthorn, Dullbriar joked, "That's as obvious as that big, red flag on your hat."

"It's an eagle feather," responded Bitterthorn.

"Never seen a red eagle," poked Long Barr.

"It had help," grumbled Bitterthorn.

"That's the Professor's mare," explained Bo as he straightened up and glanced toward the cabin. "He carries supplies to Old Fiscar every week."

Dullbriar noted Bitterthorn straightening his feather. "Forget that thing. Keep your eyes on the weeds and shadows or you'll have Seleene at your throat." He gestured down at the tracks. "Can't you see there's three set of tracks here?" Dullbriar pointed to a set of peculiar marks on the bottom of the horseshoe. "Those aren't nail marks, girls. Look closer."

"Wolf track," said Bitterthorn weakly as he stroked his short beard, "and it's directly over the horse tracks."

"Fairweather then looked up at the others. "That means that Seleene was here sometime after the Professor."

"Come." He snatched Bitterthorn's hat from his hands and plopped it down on the young dwarf's head. "Let us get to the shack and check with Old Fiscar. Maybe he can give us some advice on when we should set our trap."

"Trap?" asked Fairweather. Noting Bitterthorn smiling, he added, "Did I miss somethin' a minute ago?"

"Nothin' important," grumbled Bitterthorn. "We've decided to go and kill the black witch."

"Ibenus?" His squinty-eyed gaze fixed on Bo.

"Now, now." Long Bar patted his back. "She walks on four legs now and not two. Besides, we're five dwarves against one wolf."

Fairweather rolled his eyes as Bo continued toward the shack. "You know I can't hear. You should speak up when it concerns somethin' important."

Bitterthorn smiled.

In less than twenty minutes or so, Bo slowed, holding up his hand for the others to do the same. A bramble thicket had grown itself across the path, yielding just enough room to pass one at a time. Beyond it, and on a slight rise, was the dull yellow thatched roof of Fiscar's old shack.

Bo looked back at Long Barr and whispered, "Dullbriar and I will take a look. Keep Bitterthorn and his hat here. That feather sticks out like a goldenrod in a turnip patch."

As the two eased through the narrow opening, Bo slowed. Looking back at Dullbriar, he said in the same quiet tone, "Someone's in the front yard. I can hear 'em doin' somethin'."

The two crept up to the far edge of the thicket and stopped to watch the old dwarf. He was cutting the knee-high grass with a scythe. Several large piles easily explained why his shirt was wringing wet. The old fellow's crumpled, round-brimmed hat did its best to cover his mostly bald head, but his full beard and mustache showed not a sign of leaving him. His big, dark brown, bulbous nose nestled into his mustache looking like the abandoned egg of some delinquent bird. Swinging the scythe with the energy of a younger man, he worked diligently on finishing the lower part of his yard.

"It's just him," said Bo as he started to stand.

"Just a minute," Dullbriar grabbed Bo's right arm. "Let Bitterthorn go and announce our comin'."

Bo squinted. "I'm not so sure that's a good—"

"Sure it is," interrupted Dullbriar. "Just think of it as a learnin' moment."

"Absolutely," agreed Bo with a bit of a smile.

Bo turned and motioned for the others to join them. "Shhh," he hissed at the approaching dwarves. "We don't want to scare him now," he fixed his gaze on Bitterthorn. "Go gently now and announce our presence."

"And be sure to say it loudly," instructed Dullbriar with a grin. "He's as deaf as Fairweather."

"Nice touch," whispered Bo, watching Bitterthorn working his way between them and the brambles.

"Wait a minute," cautioned Fairweather, placing his hand on Bo's right arm. "Old Fiscar will—"

"Shhh," hissed Dullbriar. "It'll be just fine."

"But Bitterthorn won't," replied Fairweather quietly.

Stepping up behind the old dwarf with the scythe, Bitterthorn could readily see he was still proud. His clothes, although a bit tattered, had been well patched and creased. His old, brown hat had seen better days, but it still looked clean and brushed. Bitterthorn's five-foot height had him by at least a head, but there was something about Old Fiscar's rhythm with the scythe, noted the young dwarf. It didn't waver at all.

Then, stopping a shade under two steps from the old fellow, Bitterthorn he raised his voice. "Help you with that?"

In one, continuous motion, the old dwarf's next swing carried the scythe through the grass, around his left side, and then right at the younger dwarf's head.

"Wait! Wait!" shouted Bitterthorn as he dropped to his knees.

The scythe blade passed just above his hat, taking off over half the feather thereon. Then, stopping as quickly as if it had hit a tree, the head of the cutting tool came back, striking the young dwarf in the center of his chest.

"Dullbriar!" shouted Bitterthorn. He fell back to the grass behind him with the point of the scythe resting just below his chin.

"You're not Dullbriar!" snapped the old dwarf as he checked the yard at its edges. His clear, blue eyes squinted at the younger dwarf. "You got 'a be a fool, sneakin' up on me like that." He looked closer at the one before him. "You ain't Bumpas or the Professor, and you shure ain't Seleene."

"No Sir. No Sir," responded Bitterthorn as he glanced back at the plum thicket with every word.

Old Fiscar lifted the scythe's tip, but then turned the blade sideways and placed it gently back upon the young dwarf's chest.

Looking toward where the young dwarf was staring, he shouted, "Come out of there—you who would jest with this yearling's life."

Fairweather slowly stood, glaring down at Bo. "Told ya'. It's a wonder the lad didn't get marked."

Bo stood with Dullbriar. "Let 'em up, Edmond. We need your help."

The old dwarf removed the top edge of the scythe from Bitterthorn's chest, looked back up at Bo, and then stepped back with a bit of a smile. "Stop laughin'. Who is this one?"

"That's Bitterthorn," explained Bo. "He's learning under Dullbriar."

"Dyin' under him likely," mumbled the old fellow as he reached for Bitterthorn's hand and then helped him to his feet with one quick jerk. Turning back at Bo he asked, "Why so many archers? Have you sunk to huntin' in groups?"

"Maybe," admitted Bo with a shrug. "Could you stand a little comp'ny?"

"Never get enough," answered Old Fiscar as he attempted to brush off the back of the dodging dwarf's jacket. Failing to keep up with him, old dwarf added, "How's boiled taters, cabbage, and ham sound to you?"

"Wonderful," admitted Bitterthorn, now a bit distracted by the piece of feather in his hand.

Old Fiscar smiled broadly. "Well, come on to the cabin then. We'll have a bite to eat while we figure out how to put that red thing back on the yearling's hat."

As they walked toward the little shack, Bitterthorn fell back to where Dullbriar was walking and then nodded toward the two, front windows of the old shack. They had four, apple-sized crystals of amethyst sitting on each of their sills.

Dullbriar smiled as he replied, "There's two or three right at the front door, and he even has one around his neck."

"Is this because of the witch?" whispered Bitterthorn.

Dullbriar shrugged. "We'll find out directly I guess."

Noting the smoke rising from the chimney, Dullbriar watched as Old Fiscar kicked the stones aside, opened the front door, and then motioned for them to follow. Bitterthorn, watching as the boards of the old porch gave and squeaked, carefully picked out his steps to the front door.

"Mercy," complained Bitterthorn as he batted his eyes and placed his right index finger under his nose.

"Pepper'n cabbage," replied Dullbriar with a chuckle. "He has a yen for the spice."

"Just hope there's more cabbage than pepper," whispered Bitterthorn, wiping his watering eyes.

"Smells good, huh?" bragged Old Fiscar. He walked over to

the fireplace, picked up a curved poker, and then swung a pumpkin-sized, covered, iron pot from over the fire. "The Professor showed me how to make sweet corned bread to," he removed the pot's lid.

Bitterthorn managed a weak nod as he watched the steam escape from the pot. The scent of the boiled ham and cabbage pleased the dwarf. But with his nose burning and his eyes watering, he slowly backed up toward the open front door.

Dullbriar, holding his ground in front of Bitterthorn, watched Bo, Long Barr, and Fairweather intently. The first two were on either side of Old Fiscar. Not wanting to hurt his feelings, they stood still, but not so with Fairweather. The old fellow backed past Dullbriar to join Bitterthorn just inside the front door.

"Peel the potatoes, Bo," suggested Old Fiscar as he took a wooden spoon from atop a towel on the hearth and stirred the cabbage. "I got a couple of fat, yellow onions and a big, iron fry pan in the cupboard. We'll fry 'em up nice and brown with them potatoes."

"That'll help," said Bo as he and Long Barr all but raced to the far corner of the room where the burlap bag was sitting.

Just to the right of the bag, and under the only window on that side, stood a round table with four chairs. To the left of the bag was a strange, wooden box about five feet wide, two feet deep, and three feet tall.

Long Barr elbowed Bo as they fished the potatoes from the sack. "What's that?" he whispered, nodding toward the box.

"Salt box. It's another thing the Professor taught 'em and he's got 'er down to an art form. You'll see in the mornin' I hope. He'll pull out a slab of side meat, slice it good and thin, and then fry it up to a crisp fair-the-well."

As the two laid the potatoes on the table, there came a question from across the room that quickly changed the subject and the mood.

"What of all these amethyst stones?" Dullbriar took one from the window sill and held it in plain view for the others. "There's four on the sills of every window, several around the front door, a few in the edges of the fireplace, and there's a whole basket of 'em sittin' on the left side of the hearth.

Smiling at Dullbriar, the old dwarf picked up a pan, handed it to Long Barr, and then nodded toward the back door. "There's a pump just to the left of the porch. Wash 'em first." He glanced at Dullbriar.

Still 'chasing the rabbit', Dullbriar asked, "Can you hear the witch when the wolf comes."

"Just as I feared," mumbled the old dwarf as he plopped the spoon back onto the towel. He turned, stepped around the basket of stones and stopped in front of a tall cabinet. Slowly shaking his head, he opened one of the lower doors and pulled out a half-gallon jug with a cork in its mouth. Pulling the cork, he took a long pull from it, and handed it to Dullbriar. "You've finally come for the witch, haven't you?"

"Yes, sir," replied Dullbriar, eagerly taking the jug.

As Dullbriar hoisted the jug, Old Fiscar looked at Bo. "Did you get the Council's approval on this?"

"Don't need it. Ibenus is a clear and eminent danger now and she's worked her last spell."

"Can't say's I'm sorry," admitted Old Fiscar. He pulled the jug loose from Dullbriar and handed it to Bitterthorn. "I've been collectin' rocks ever since the Professor had at her," he admitted. "You'll have to kill Seleene, you know. And when you do, you best be wearin' one of 'em cause when the wolf dies, the witch will have at one of you. The only way she can stay alive in this realm is to get into one of you within two minutes or so. Any longer and the Shadows will come for her."

"Get Bitterthorn out of the jug, Long Bar," instructed Bo. "You don't want dulled senses this close to the pond." He turned back to Old Fiscar. "When and where should we wait for her?"

The old dwarf glanced out of the window next to the cabinet. "She comes to and from the pond twice a week I'd say, and most times late evening' to midnight. But you'll get a better shot when she taunts me right out there in front of the porch steps. You can wait for her in the plum thicket." He turned his attention back to Dullbriar. "Your answer is yes. I can hear her talk to me, and when she does, I can't get her out of my head. She has three more to kill—Bo, the Professor, and some young girl named Helen."

"My turn at the jug," grumbled Bitterthorn as he watched Fairweather's attempt to drain it.

"Enough of this witch stuff!" Fairweather shoved the jug into

Bitterthorn's waiting arms. "I'll get the pan ready and start brownin' these onions. Have those potatoes ready when I call for 'em." He gestured at Long Bar. "Stay away from that jug when you're usin' your knife. Wouldn't want you losin' a thumb."

~ * ~

Later that evening, Dullbriar retired to two, padded chairs he had pulled together facing each other by the fireplace. Since the jug was all but a memory, Old Fiscar took to his single bed by the window left of the front door. Bitterthorn made up a pallet close to the hearth and away from the other dwarves in the middle of the cabin. He laughed silently at Dullbriar every time the dwarf made a face at the *others* breaking wind.

"What time is it?" whispered Dullbriar.

Bitterthorn shrugged his shoulders and mouthed, *No clock*. He whispered, "I'd guess somewhere around eleven or so." He propped up on one elbow. "Can't sleep. Keep thinkin' about what we're fixin' to do."

"Shhh," hissed Dullbriar. "I think I heard someone say something.

"It's Old Fiscar," whispered Bitterthorn. "He's not sleepin' well. Done kicked his cover off."

"Leave me alone," grumbled the old fellow as he rolled away from the window.

Bo, the closest dwarf to Fiscar's bed, slowly sat up, rubbing the sleep from his eyes. "What's botherin' Fiscar?" he kept his voice low.

"Thinks somebody's tryin' to get in," replied Long Barr as he sat up on his blanket and nodded over at Fairweather, who was still asleep.

Bo slowly shook his head and whispered, "Leave him be. There's not a soul out there. That old porch creeks like an old oak in the wind and I ain't heard a squeak from it."

"Shhh," hissed Dullbriar again. He kicked his blanket off and then rolled from his chair bed to the floor. Motioning toward the floor, he mouthed, *Under-the-house*.

Then, from the direction of Old Fiscar's bed, came what sounded like a dire warning.

"She's callin' your name, Bo Bumpas," said Old Fiscar sternly.

Seeing the old dwarf now wide awake and sitting up in his bed, the others—all but Fairweather—slowly looked down at the small cracks in the floor, trying to see into the darkness below.

Noting the old dwarf had shut his eyes and was now holding his ears, Bitterthorn pointed at him and whispered, "He hears somethin', Bo. Get him to tell us what he hears."

"I heard ya," grumbled Old Fiscar. "It's Ibenus. The wolf is with us. The witch said, three left. Bo Bumpas, you're next."

"Why only three?" asked Long Barr, looking at Bo.

Bo sat back up on his quilt, glanced at Long Barr, and then looked back down at the cracks in the floor. "The night the Professor shot her with his wee pistol, we had went to her home to confront her about tryin' to take a child. The child was Tulip, the daughter of Hayslip Torpe. Her husband, Ruben, was a heavy drinker and Hayslip had run him off for the last time." Bo looked up at Long Barr. "I think Ruben hired Ibenus to steal Tulip away from Hayslip. Anyways, Tulip was six years old and proved a bit too much to handle for the old hag. That gave Hayslip and the neighbors' time to band together and run her off."

"So, she's out for revenge?" guessed Bitterthorn.

"No. She's been run off by others before that, but this was the last straw for the dwarves. Hackenbrier, bein' the Council Leader, took the Professor and me to her shack for a final confrontation. Hackenbrier gave her the order to leave without so much as a word of explanation. In her anger, she pulled a dagger on me, and the Professor shot her. We just stood there in shock and watched her die. In her last throws, she reached out for Hackenbrier we thought, but Seleene was right behind him. A dark shadow then blew between Bo and Hack. Before we could figure out what just happened, the wolf pounced on Hack, tore his throat out, and then bounded off into the woods. The Professor shot at it twice more but missed."

"So…" mused Bitterthorn, "She's after Bo and the Professor, but who's the third?

Everyone then turned to Old Fiscar, awaiting an answer to the puzzle.

"Don't know her," the old dwarf responded quickly. "Called her Helen, she did. Said somethin' 'bout a friend of Bo."

"She's our Bright Helen, you misfits—the Professor's grand-child." explained Bo. "She stood with me against Seleene not long ago. I guess, through the wolf's eyes, she noticed the girl's aura."

Snapping his fingers, Bitterthorn exclaimed, "I've got it! The old hag noticed an old enemy."

"An eventual one," corrected Dullbriar.

At that very comment, something ran from under the old shack, bumping the floor as it went.

"Sufferin' ghosts!" Bitterthorn cried out as all but Fairweather scrambled to get off the floor.

Fairweather jumped, awaken by the shaking floor, and then struggled to a sitting position on his blanket. Slowly looking around the room, he noticed Bo and his friends were on tables, chairs, or atop the hearth. His gaze fixed on Bo. "Why do I have the feelin' I missed somethin' again?"

"She's gone," replied Long Barr. "Went east, toward the plum thicket."

"Toward the creek and then to Gossamer Swamp for the Hobs is more like it," Dullbriar ran to the front window right of the door. "We'll lay for her in the plum thicket tomorrow night. I don't see her at all. Let's get some sleep for now. We're gon'na need it."

Rubbing his face briskly, Fairweather, grumbled, "You hard-heads woke me up to see you standin' on anything but the floor, and now you tell me to go back to sleep? What the devil has just happened?"

"We had comp'ny," explained Bitterthorn, "but she was too bashful to come in."

"Good grief," grumbled Old Fiscar as he settled back to his bed and then rolled toward the window, leaving Bitterthorn trying to coax the last drop from the jug.

~ * ~

The light of the next morning came in loudly through the thin drapes of the old cabin's front windows. With a rooster crow-ing from somewhere in the back yard, the dwarves slowly started to come to life…

"Ohhh, my head," complained Fairweather as Bo bumped his feet. "Them boots are hard. You just bumped one o' my corns."

"Get up, Sunshine," exclaimed Bo loudly, nudging his feet again. "For an older brother, you should set a better example. We're gettin' planted out there in the plum thicket before evenin'."

"Why so early?" grumbled Bitterthorn, puzzling over only one sock he was holding up.

"Simple." Bo poured some water into a washbowl sitting on the table. "If Seleene comes a bit early, we'll be ready. "I'll be right out there on the front porch with sword in belt, waitin' for her."

Long Barr hesitated with his first boot half on and turned his attention to Old Fiscar. "From which direction does she come? I don't want that wolf sneakin' up on any of us."

"South," replied Old Fiscar as he plopped a slab of salted meat on the cutting table. "Always from the yellow grass and the Hobs. She'll pause right out there in the yard with her paws on the porch steps, stopped only by the stones."

Picking up one of the smaller stones, Fairweather asked, "What about these stones next to the hearth? Wouldn't you think it wise for us to take some of em' with us?"

"No, I wouldn't," the old dwarf shook his head. "She'll sense that and know somethin's afoot."

"He's right," Long Barr looked at Fairweather. "Lose all of em.'"

"We're gon'na be geese on a table," grumbled Fairweather as he pulled two stones from his pants pockets.

Bo quickly turned toward him. "We've no choice. If this is to be successful, we'll need to get her with the first volley. If she's wounded, I'll finish her with my short sword."

Bitterthorn slowly shook his head as he put his shirt on. "I've seen Seleene up close. She was eye to eye with me and I was standin' at the time. One snap and you're history."

Whistling across the room, something banged against the wall only inches from where Bitterthorn was standing. Long Barr walked over toward the young dwarf, glared at him, and then pulled his axe from the wall. "We're dwarves for cryin' out loud! If you're afraid, you can stay here and cover yourselves with Fiscar's rocks. The rest of us will take care of the wolf."

Bitterthorn slowly turned, pulled two amethyst crystals from his pockets, and then let them fall back into Fiscar's sack. Sleepily, Fairweather did the same.

"Good." He patted Fairweather on the back and then added, "This afternoon, we'll take our places in the plum thicket. Right now, Fiscar's carvin' on that meat. I'm gon'na take Bitterthorn out back to the chicken coop and let him distract that old red rooster while I steal an egg or two."

~ * ~

Later that evening, Old Fiscar passed out sacks of cut ham, corned bread, and cold, boiled potatoes to Long Barr, Fairweather, Bitterthorn, and Dullbriar as they lined up by the front door.

Standing at the doorway, Bo instructed, "Pick your places carefully in the plum thicket where you can't be seen from the house. I'll be sittin' in plain sight on the front porch with Fiscar. Seleene will come up from the south and we'll back up behind the stones. Wait until she pauses at the steps before you let fly, and don't miss."

Bitterthorn gave a half smile at Bo. "That little fae would come in handy right now. Where is she?"

"She's with my wife and the girls. Those three need her more than we do."

Then, as the dwarves found their places in the thicket, Bo spotted a flock of partridges that were flushed from the grass just a bit south of the shack. He stood quickly, watching the scrub and pine saplings of the thicket. As he was about to take his seat again, a muffled sound came from the field.

Old Fiscar eased to the edge of his seat. Glancing at the still standing Bo, he whispered, "Hear that?"

"Sounded like a low growl," replied Bo.

"The wind's shifted. I can feel it on my left cheek and blowing right toward that field." Fiscar cast a glance at Bo. "Where are they?"

"Don't point and I'll tell you," He kept his voice soft. Knowing that loud sounds and careless gestures were enemies of the moment, Bo pulled his pipe from his jacket. As he fished about for his tobacco pouch, he softly replied, "See that big oak tree on your right, just at the south side of the thicket?"

Turning his back from the direction of the growl, Fiscar answered, "I do."

"Bitterthorn is there. Dullbriar is at the huge stone just north of the tree. Long Barr, our best marksman, is about even with us, and Fairweather is at the north end of the thicket. If she gets by and runs that way, he'll get a shot at her again."

Before Bo could say another word, a scream erupted from somewhere near the old oak. Dropping his pipe and pouch, Bo stood, pulled his sword. Then, with his stomach knotting up, he eased toward the porch steps. "Where did that come from?"

"Don't rightly know."

The two eased from the porch, searching the thicket for movement of any kind.

"Bitterthorn!" screamed Bo as the young dwarf stumbled into view.

Unable to answer, the young dwarf held tightly to his bleeding throat. Then, with blood dripping from his elbows, he fell face down into the grass.

"Take this," said Old Fiscar, throwing him the bow and quiver.

"Bitterthorn!" Bo screamed, shoved his sword back into its sheath, and ran from the porch toward his wounded friend. With a quick glance back at Old Fiscar. "Get back behind the amethysts! Seleene is here."

"I never saw her!" Dullbriar bounded from the grass by the stone. "This just can't be." He fell to his knees by Bitterthorn's motionless body.

The huge pool of blood was reason enough to know that their friend was no longer with them. If there had been any doubt then, the gaping hole where his Adam's apple once was silenced it.

"Over here! She's over here in the woods!" shouted Long Barr as Dullbriar pulled Bitterthorn into his lap.

With clinched fists, Bo turned toward where Long Barr had shouted. "Stay with him," he growled at Dullbriar, pulling an arrow from its sheath, "but keep your wits about you or the witch will be havin' at you also."

Bo turned, and with sword in hand, he muscled his way through the plum thicket toward where he last heard Long Barr. Briars pulled at his jacket and pants and tore at his face and hands but he felt nothing. Not seeing Seleene as he pushed from the far side of the thicket, he searched for Long Barr.

"Over here, Bo" shouted Long Barr.

Now, running a bit north of the stone, Bo noted Long Barr facing a waist-high thicket with arrow to string.

"She went in there." He pointed toward an opening in the thicket. "I sent an arrow right in behind her and heard her yelp, but I don't know where I hit her."

"Maybe you slowed her a bit."

"How's Bitterthorn?" asked Long Barr, watching the thicket closely.

Bo slowly shook his head. "He didn't make it, Long. Seleene tore his throat out. I'm afraid this is going to go badly for us."

Looking as if the strength had just been sapped right out of his body, Long Barr let the tension off his bow and lowered it in front of him.

"She's just beat us again," added Bo.

"Not if I can get another shot," grumbled Long Barr, raising his bow back up. "I'll strangle her with my bowstring if I have to." Long Barr slowly shook his head in disgust. "He was probably day dreamin' like most young dwarves and didn't hear the wolf sneak up on..." Long Barr's eyes then grew big as he grabbed Bo's arm. "Fairweather! Go check on him right now! "Get him out of the thicket and back on the porch where he at least see. I'll watch the clearin' between the woods and the thicket while you go."

With arrow set to the string and his attention on the edge of the woods to his right, Bo ran as fast as he was able toward his brother. As he circled around the little finger of stunted spruce trees where his brother was supposed to be, he all but lost his breath. There, beneath the outside trees, was a motionless brown lump of color showing above of the short grass.

"No-no-no!" He gripped his arrow alongside of his bow and then pulled his sword from its sheath.

Throwing caution aside, he ran straight to his brother. Brushing the tears from his eyes, he dropped his bow, took a quick look around, and then fell to his knees beside the face down body. With his gaze drawn to the puncture holes in the turned up collar of his brother's heavy jacket, Bo slowly reached his hand out toward it.

"Fairweather?" he said softly. Pulling back the collar, he noticed his bruised and scratched neck. "Fairweather!" he cried and rolled his brother into his arms.

The dwarf opened his eyes, smiled for a short moment, and then slowly closed them.

"This way," shouted Dullbriar.

Looking up, Bo could see the younger dwarf carrying Bitterthorn toward the cabin with Old Fiscar in the yard, covering them with his bow.

"The wolf's in the thicket Long Barr!" shouted Old Fiscar

"I'm comin'," said Bo weakly as he lifted his brother and trotted toward the old shack.

The quiver in Bo's reply might have been the cause for Dullbriar to look back but he continued toward the shack. "Don't falter now, old friend," added Dullbriar loudly.

"In here," instructed Old Fiscar as Dullbriar stepped onto the porch with Bitterthorn.

Old Fiscar looked back at Bo. "Bring him on. Bring him and be quick about it. She's probably watchin' us right now."

"Long Barr hit her," added Bo. He quickly stepped onto the porch and entered the cabin. Easing his brother to the floor, he struggled to keep his emotions under control. "Check Bitterthorn first. He looks in a bad way."

After a moment with Old Fiscar on his knees by Bitterthorn, the old dwarf looked at Bo and Dullbriar and slowly shook his head. "Nothin' I can do for the yearling. He's gone for sure. How 'bout this one?" he nodded at Fairweather.

"I think I scared Seleene off before she could finish what she had started, but he was out when I got to him," explained Bo.

"There's a pail of water by the stove," Fiscar waved a hand at the stove. "Fetch it and rags from the cupboard. Bring the salve in the blue jar next to them."

While Bo went for the cupboard, Dullbriar walked over to the open door and looked toward the plum thicket.

"Where's Long Barr?" asked Old Fiscar as he removed Fairweather's jacket.

Bo glanced at Dullbriar. "When I last saw him, he was on the far side of the thicket, daring Seleene to show herself."

Fairweather groaned.

"Still alive I see," Old Fiscar grinned. "Took 'em down by the right arm," the old dwarf noted the fang marks on Fairweather's upper left arm. "Clean through. That's where the blood's comin' from." He glanced up at Bo. "Put the pail and the salve right by me. You've got a lucky brother, you have. If he didn't have that collar turned up, he'd be dead by now."

"Didn't hear her at all," the injured dwarf struggled to explain. "Felt like a tree fell on me. When I came to, I was lookin' at Bo."

"So good to have you back," replied Bo.

"Enough of the niceties," grumbled Old Fiscar as he helped Fairweather remove his shirt. Growling, he warned "If you don't want me to be doin' this with another one, you two best be out that door and fetch that hard-headed Long Barr away from that witch!"

"Yes, Sir," replied Bo, looking down at his brother.

"Go on," said Fairweather as the old dwarf applied a white salve to his upper arm. "I'll be all right now."

Old Fiscar reached into his pants pocket, produced a hen's-egg sized amethyst, and then held it out to Bo.

"No thanks," managed Bo as he backed toward the door. "I'll have to use the same reason Long Barr is using now—I want her to come close just one more time." He kicked a wooden chair across the room. "Stay with these two, Dullbriar. They might need another bow."

"I will, but be careful what you wish for," Dullbriar warned as Bo left the cabin.

Running the short distance to where he found his brother, Bo picked up his bow and arrow and headed to the clearing on the far side. Long Barr had remained where he'd left him and Bo trotted in that direction.

"Shhh," hissed Long Barr as he approached. "She's crossed back into the scrub. I can't see her, but she makes just enough noise now and then to let me know she's there. I guess two against one might not suit her now."

"Taunting us." Bo shifted his gaze to Long Barr and asked, "Do we have a plan?"

"Staying alive," Long Barr smirked without taking his gaze off the scrub only six paces from them. "How is your brother?"

"Shook up a bit. Seleene had at him." The dwarf then raised his voice. "But I robbed her of another victim!"

"She's still in there," said Long Barr with a smile. "Let's finish

this if we can. We'll leave here and head for the yellow grass. Between here and there is a fairly open field. She won't chance that.
She knows I can hit her. She'll have to cross the creek and enter
the woods beyond." As they moved away, Long Barr continued.
"When we get over that little rise up ahead, we'll swap clothes and
shoes and split up. You've got big feet, so your shoes will fit I
think. We're about the same size in the chest, but your pants will
be a mite short. But at that distance, she's not likely to notice.
We'll also be upwind of her and she won't smell us. She'll have to
hunt by sight. She will be after you, but will find me beneath the
cliffs instead. You cross the creek where it meanders through the
stones and get above her. That'll be an easy shot for you but wait
until I get one off first. Keep even with me and watch my back.
She won't see you because of the cliff, but we can see each other.
If I didn't wound her too badly, this will work well."

"Agreed," replied Bo as they picked up the pace.

As the two topped the little rise, Long Barr looked back.
"We'll change here." After taking a few more steps, he stopped,
sat on the grass, and started pulling at his shoes. "I got a glimpse
at her. She was at the creek and chewing at her haunches, but
she's slowly coming nonetheless. Let's get our clothes switched."

Bo, kicking off his shoes, looked toward the creek. "It makes
a bend away from us right where we are and just before the crossing. She won't see me."

After the two had exchanged clothes, they all but ran around
the bend in the creek. Pausing at the rocky ford, Long Barr said,
"Cross quickly. Get up there as fast as you can. Remember, she's
in the woods on your side, but the woods are thick between you
two. I'll make sure she sees me. She'll cross to my side and that's
where we'll have at her."

"Done," agreed Bo. He wheeled around and ran toward the
crossing.

Picking his way across the stones, he watched the woods, but
saw no sign of the wolf. With his collar up high and Long Barr's
hat pulled down to his eyebrows, Bo pressed on and up the incline
toward the top of the cliffs.

Well past noon, thought Bo as he stopped to check the direction of the wind. *Blowin' from the south. That's good. Need to get this
done before nightfall.*

After gaining the top of the grade, Bo paused to look back once more, but could see no sign of the wolf. Pulling his bow from his shoulder, he put an arrow to the string, and then eased forward in the knee-high brush. He had only gone a few yards when he spotted something furry through the weeds at the base of a young oak. It was directly in front of him.

Now what? He eased forward.

Nearing the sapling, he noted a bit of brown color on its far left side. "All right, Seleene, let's do this," he murmured to himself. He started a slow circle around the left side of the sapling.

Then, when only three paces from the fir, a loud blowing sound erupted from behind it. The air filled with brown fur and the white tail of a large doe.

"Geeze!" exclaimed Bo as he released his arrow. Watching the weak shot pass under the leaping doe, the dwarf noticed she wasn't looking at him at all, but more to his left and back a ways.

Wiping the sweat from his brow with his jacket sleeve, Bo slowly turned. His heart all but stopped. There, barely eight paces from him, stood Seleene—the nightmare he had relived time and again ever since Ibenus had brought the wolf into his life. Now, with his sword in its sheath and no arrow at the bow, the dwarf pondered his next move. The wolf just stared calmly at him awaiting that very decision. Bo could see her slightly raised, left foot and the two-inch stubble of a shaft sticking out, high on her left hip.

"Guess we're past talkin', ain't we, Ibenus," Bo let cold resolution sink into his voice.

With that, Bo reached with his right hand across his belt buckle for his sword. Unsheathing it was the best he could do, for the wolf was on him in two bounds.

"Eat this!" Bo shouted, jamming the bow crossways in the wolf's jaws.

The jolt from the wolf's attack and the fall to the ground, loosed the sword from the dwarf's hand. Now, with no way to make another stand, and his sword a bit too far to reach, Bo held to the bow and then managed to kick her away from him.

Quickly pulling his dagger, Bo growled, "Come, and bring your ugly face to me again and this old dagger will find your black heart before I die."

The dwarf brandished his double-edged knife and then watched as the wolf dropped the bow from her jaws. Faster than the dwarf had given her credit, Seleene lunged forward, but instead of getting too close to the knife, she grabbed the dwarf's left leg, just above his boot.

"Ieee! Foul creature!" shouted the dwarf as the wolf began to drag him toward the cliff.

Grasping at anything he could and kicking with his right foot, Bo finally managed to sit up and stab at Seleene's head. Fortunately, that one effort got the blade in just under the wolf's left eye. Yelping in pain, Seleene leaped backwards, looked at the dwarf, and then north from where Bo had just come. Then, without a moment's hesitation, she bounded off toward the woods and Gossamer Swamp.

After watching her for a moment, it was all the dwarf could do to crawl through the grass and grab his sword.

"Bo! Bo!" shouted Long Barr from down the incline a little.

Lying back, Bo listened to his friend run toward him. "I'm fine," he managed as he lay flat of his back, waving his sword back and forth.

"Are you hurt?" asked Long Barr as he ran up.

"Ohhh no," Bo chuckled. "I'm just restin' after climbin' all the way up here only to find Seleene waitin'. I got a bit distracted by a deer. When I finally got my heart beatin' again, I was eyeball to eyeball with her." He then stared at Long Barr and added, "She tagged me, but I drew a bit of her blood. She may be blinded in her left eye."

Long Barr noted his torn and bloody pants leg. "Can you stand?"

"I can run if she comes back," Bo smirked and forced himself to stand, but favored his left leg badly. "I don't think it's broke, but it hurts like the devil." Looking at Long Barr, he added, "Can't make it back to Old Fiscar's. Go get the Professor by way of the Oak Gate. It'll take you right into his home."

Long Barr knelt down, pulled out his dagger, and then slit open Bo's left pants leg. He pulled out a small canister from his coat pocket and poured some of its contents directly on the wound.

"Ooooowwww!" screamed Bo. "Why didn't you just set fire

to it?" he grumbled as Long Barr tied his bandanna around it.

Long Barr placed his hand on the toe of Bo's boot. "Push on it for me."

Bo grimaced but managed it. "Not broken."

"True, but it may be cracked. You need to stay off it for a while." He looked up at Bo. "Not going inside. Never going inside the home of a man again. Besides, that'll leave you in the woods with Seleene and I'll lose another friend." Not waiting for a comment, the strong dwarf stood and picked up Bo like a sack of potatoes. "I'll go by Fiscar's Pond, but first, I'll put you in a safe spot. It's one of the places I've set up to use if I get caught out in the night."

"Seleene's wounded twice now." Bo grimaced, but held his leg as still as possible. "Perhaps she'll forget about this for a while."

"Perhaps. Perhaps not. The old tree's not far north of here. I'll get you up in it and then you'll be safe."

Pushing on north, Bo soon noticed Long Barr was paying more attention to the woods to the east than usual. "You're watchin' somethin' aren't you?" Bo looked also, but could see not a thing.

"Not real sure. Thought I saw the wolf, but this thing's not quite big enough. Besides, it's the strangest shade of orange I've ever seen."

Long Barr then slowed to a stop. "Rest your weight on your right foot and hold to this old tree." he lowered Bo to the grass.

Wincing and hobbling, Bo looked up into the old white oak. The top of it had been torn out by a storm. Plus, lightning had all but gutted it, leaving an enormous hole down through its middle and out its west side. It seemed to be supporting itself by huge limbs that were actually imbedded and growing in the ground.

"Will you look at this." Long Barr walked closer to one of the near limbs. "The old tree is defying death by re-rootin' itself and…"

Bo's words trailed off as he looked out into the woods, a bit north of the tree.

"See 'em?" whispered Long Barr, looking in the same direction.

"Just a shadow, but somethin's there nonetheless."

"Ease around this side, Bo," instructed Long Barr. "There's a twelve-foot ladder in there and a platform you can almost lay down on."

Looking at the puddle of red next to his left boot, Bo said, "My bleedin's brought the wolf back to us I'm afraid. I'll bet Ibenus hasn't allowed her to hunt lately. She must be starvin'."

"Don't think on that," snapped Long Barr. "Come quickly." Dropping his bow and quiver to the grass, he helped his friend inside the yawning oak. "I need to get you up that ladder. I don't fancy facin' Seleene if she corners me in the bottom of this old tree."

With Long Barr on the ladder beneath him, Bo struggled one step at a time to within reach of the platform.

"Hurry up," encouraged Long Barr as he supported Bo's hurt leg. "You're bleedin' again. I'm tryin' to save the Valkyrie a trip. Use a sock or somethin' to redo that bandage when you get on the boards."

"All right. All right. I'm tryin'. I'm tryin,'" grumbled Bo as he hoisted himself up toward the platform.

Finally, as Bo took hold of the platform's edge, something rustled the scrub somewhere outside the old tree.

"Sufferin' turnips," complained Long Barr loudly. "Somethin's sneakin' up on me and you're all but sittin' on my face. I can't see a thing."

Then, as Bo finally pulled himself from the dwarf's shoulder, Long Barr pulled his sword from its sheath and jumped to the ground. Spinning around, he faced the opening and whatever was outside.

Long Barr's eyes grew big as saucers, as he stared at the unknown creature. Not two feet from the opening of the old tree, stood an orange and white, doglike animal. It had a long snout, big fuzzy ears, and a head as big as a wolf.

"You big baby," it quipped with its tongue hanging from the left side of its mouth. "Haven't you ever seen a faerie mount?"

"Who is that?" asked Bo from the pedestal. "That voice sounds familiar."

Long Barr, still staring at the animal, only cocked his head sideways a bit. The movement was instantly mimicked by the doglike creature. Then, looking a bit closer, Long Barr caught a movement between the animal's ears. There sat the source of the dog's voice.

"Rosebud!" exclaimed the dwarf. "You scared me out of a full-year's-growth.

"Nope," disagreed the fae. "Zee did that without even knowing it. The little fae glanced at the dwarf's bow and quiver in the grass near the tree. "He had you stone cold, didn't he?"

"Yes," grumbled Long Barr as he shoved his sword back in its sheath, making a distinct click before he spoke to Bo. "Are you all right?"

"Just peachy," grumbled Bo. "I think I got the bleedin' stopped."

Rosebud stood. "What did you two do? What happened to Bo? Why is he stuck up in a hollow tree?"

Long Bar scuffed his right foot on the ground. "Tried to kill Seleene, misjudged the witch, and we came out on the sticky end of the stick again. We lost Bitterthorn and almost Bo's brother. Bo was the last one she had at and we're none the better for it."

Hearing that, Rosebud shot right past Long Barr and up in the old tree. "I'll get some soap root to wash it off, a poultice with cure-all leaves to help heal it, and willow bark for a tea will keep the fever down!" She looked down at Long Bar. "You go by way of the White Oak Door and fetch the Professor."

"Told 'em that I did," grumbled Bo, "but he just wouldn't listen."

"Not going inside a man's house," insisted Long Barr.

As quick as a cat's sneeze, the fae shot from the old tree's opening, ending up only a reach from Long's bulbous nose. Then, poking his nose to emphasize her anger, she spoke. "Fiscar's-Pond-is-too-far-away. Most who use the shift-a-robe do it because they think on the shift-a-robe. Have you been to the Professor's cottage?"

"Of course."

"Do you remember the huge ash at the lower end of his back yard?"

"Yes, I do."

"Think on that and you'll walk out of the north side of its bark."

"That's a gate?" asked Long Barr with no little interest.

"Only on the north side and push through the old, hollow tree with your left hand only while you're thinking on the ash."

"Long Barr's eyes squinted at her as he paused a bit. "You're not tryin' to get even with me for that Mason jar thing last month are you?"

"Not yet," snapped Rosebud. She pulled her dagger and placed its tip on the dwarf's nose. "But it's coming. Bo needs help right now, so get going." The little fae glanced down at the orange dog. "This is Zee. He's a corgi. There's nothing in these forests that can detect a witch or a wolf faster than he can. He'll go with you."

Long peeped inside the old oak and looked up toward Bo. "See you later, old friend," he said and then started walking.

"Watch for him, Zee," added Rosebud.

The stubby, shepherd sized dog trotted after the dwarf, watching the woods as he went.

"Better not be no faerie humor stuff," grumbled Long Barr as he walked away.

"I heard that!" warned the fae.

"Let him be, Rosebud." Closing his eyes tightly, Bo placed his hand upon his wound. "This leg is killin' me."

~ * ~

Now, with a new urgency in his step, Long Barr and the corgi called Zee, left the cliffs, crossed Gossamers Swamp at the Rocky Ford, and then continued north-west toward the Whitestone Trail. Skirting close to the Black Forest, Zee woofed his disapproval occasionally, but the dwarf saw nothing and pushed on without delay. Once at the Whitestone Trail, Long Barr paused to sit and rest under a young fir.

"Faerie mount, huh?" Bo stared at the dog.

The stout-built corgi made not a sound, only glanced at the dwarf.

"You like sausage?" asked the dwarf.

Zee knew the word, sausage, and quickly licked his chops, taking a new interest in the strange, little man.

"Let's see then," added Long Barr. He reached into his bag and pulled out two sausages and a hunk of orange bread.

Zee sat up immediately, licking his chops again. Laying a sausage and half the bread in front of his new friend, the dwarf sat back to eat his portion.

"Two, maybe three hours 'till dawn," mused the dwarf. "Mrs. Narbie is an early riser. Perhaps if we wait in the back yard, she'll see us through the big kitchen window."

Quickly finishing the food, Zee stood, walked into the double-lanes of the old road, and then looked pointedly back at the dwarf.

"I know. I know," replied Long Barr through a long yawn. "We'll go again," he decided as he struggled to his feet. Sticking the top of the bag under his belt, he joined the corgi.

Leading the way, Zee broke into a trot, following the road north, sniffing the breeze as he went. After another hour had passed, Long Barr slowed, looking at every large oak near the left side of the trail.

"Ever seen a road so straight?" he grumbled. "It seems to go on forever," he added through a long yawn.

But the corgi never slowed, just glanced back occasionally at the now-faltering dwarf. Then, just as the sun started to show itself through the trees toward the east, Zee stopped, and then stared at something on the left side of the trail.

"Thought you'd never stop," complained Long Barr. He leaned against a big pine. The dwarf let his tired, sleepy eyes follow Zee's snout out to what had his attention. "Bless my beard," he said weakly and pushed away from the pine to stare at the old white oak the fae had dubbed *Martin's Way*. "Here," the dwarf pulled the last sausage from the bag and laid it in front of the corgi. "You've earned it for sure."

As the corgi finished the sausage, Long Bar walked toward the tree with his eyes fixed on the gaping, dark hole in its side. Stopping as close as he dared, he felt something next to his right leg. Zee had sat beside him, awaiting the dwarf's next move.

"The only time I was ever in a human's house," Long Barr began with a sigh. "I was very young and very sick at the time. I got stabbed with needles, froze with ice, bled with little, hot tubes, and given something called ipecac. I almost threw up my toenails."

Zee then growled, nipping the back of his right heel.

"I'm goin'. I'm goin'!" exclaimed Long Barr, looking back into the darkness of the hollow. He closed his eyes and thought of the large tree at the end of the Professor's back yard. "Ash at the end of the yard. Ash at the end of the yard," he repeated as he extended his left hand and stepped into the darkness.

He never felt the rough wood at the back of the old oak's hollow.

Part 4
The Witch's Stick

Realizing it was Saturday, Narbie Tucker was most reluctant to leave the warm covers of her featherbed. October's chill had seeped through the partially open windows of the cabin, gifting the whole place with a cool, crisp feeling. The crowing of her old, red rooster hadn't bothered her much as well. But he was still fussing and that had now started to lay heavily on her mind.

"Martin?" softly said the little lady with a bit of a nudge to her husband.

"Just close the window," suggested Martin, not moving. "Just one more hour."

That comment brought the little lady up on one elbow to peep out the window and into the back yard.

"Gracious, Martin," she said softly. "There's a fox in the lower end of the yard and it's the biggest one I've ever…"

Her voice trailed off leaving the sleepy, old fellow guessing.

"What is it, Grandmother?" asked Helen as she peeped into the bedroom.

Martin rose up and rubbed the sleep from his eyes. "Check the back yard for a big fox, Helen. I can still hear Old Red fussing."

"And a man," added Narbie, still at the window.

Not winning by much, Helen raced her grandfather to the window on Narbie's side of the bed.

"What do you two make of that?" asked Narbie as she returned to her pillow.

"The animal's a Corgi, Grandmother." She pressed her nose against the window. "But I don't see a man."

"Corgi? No man?" queried Narbie. "No one owns a dog like that around here, and where did that little man go?"

"I'll check them out," said Helen.

She spun around and headed back to her room. Knowing her grandfather was a fast dresser; Helen quickly donned her denims and opted for a heavy, flannel shirt. *Shoes and socks,* she grabbed them and headed out of the room, down the hall, and onto the back porch.

"It *is* a corgi," she said excitedly as she tied the last shoe and then jumped from the steps. "Come here sweetie," she called softly, as she looked about the edge of the woods for the man her grandmother had seen.

Sitting at the lower edge of the yard, the orange and white corgi only moved his front feet a bit, but made no other attempt to come to her.

"Well, all right then, but don't run," said Helen softly.

But as Helen drew near, the corgi stood and trotted back into the shadows of the woods.

"No, no, no," repeated Helen softly, resisting the urge to run after it.

"Helen," called her grandfather. "You just wait right there, young lady."

"Yes, sir," Helen stopped short of the woods, peering into its shadows. "Ohhh good," she whispered, seeing the orange dog had stopped next to the silhouette of a little man.

Brushing his long, gray hair back under his deerskin hat, the figure stepped into the light. In his hand he held out a moleskin cap.

"Long, is that you?" asked Martin.

"And company," answered the dwarf.

"That's Bo's moleskin hat," mused Helen. "Where did you get it?"

"From Bo o' course. I've got 'em in a safe tree. I'm afraid Seleene had at him. Got him on the lower left leg, she did. He can hardly walk."

"You two know these people?" asked Narbie as she walked up, tying her apron about her waist.

"Ha!" exclaimed Long Barr. "People…now there's a word. Not sure I like the comparison."

Martin chuckled. Then, looking at the little man over his wire-rimmed glasses, he made the introductions. "This is Long Barr, Narbie. Long, this is my wife."

"Ma'am," replied the dwarf just above a whisper.

"Who is this?" asked Helen as she stepped forward and knelt

two paces in front of the corgi.

"That's Rosebud's friend," replied the dwarf. "Calls 'em Zee. Some kind of faerie mount or somethin'." Long Barr glanced down at the corgi. "Go to her, Zee. She's a friend."

Zee quickly glanced at the dwarf and then ran straight to Helen.

"Can one of you help us?" asked Long Barr. "Rosebud's takin' care of him now, but I'd feel a might better if one of you could come. Seleene's fangs went clean through his calf."

"We'll come," answered Helen without hesitation.

"I'll go," said Martin. His voice stern. He looked down at Helen. "Go and get my black bag. Make sure there's some gauze, alcohol, peroxide, two needles, two rolls of stitching string, and three vials of penicillin." He turned his attention to Narbie. "Please, if you will, get my Duck Hill revolver. If there's a wolf about, I want to be prepared."

"Let's go," said Narbie.

She took Helen by the hand and walked briskly for the house. Once there, Helen quickly ran to her room, opted for a pair of light boots, and then a light jacket. On her way to the pantry, she ignored her grandmother's *you're not going* expression.

"Get some extra bandages," suggested Narbie, her gaze narrowed. "There's no telling what Martin will run into once he's with those little people."

"I've got everything," said Helen, holding the black bag up at the back door as Narbie trotted down the hall toward her.

Long Barr, seeing the two returning across the lawn, nodded at Martin. "She's Bo's friend, Professor. Don't you think she should go? After all, there's not another one I know who can hear an Int."

"A what?" asked Martin.

"Uhhh…The lass is a bit more than you think, Sir. She should go with us."

"I am," agreed Helen as she and Narbie trotted up beside them.

"Ohhh, Martin," complained Narbie. "This girl's not going again is she?"

Immediately, a crashing sound came from the woods, jarring the ground.

"What was that?" queried Narbie.

"A tree probably fell," guessed Martin.

"Or showed its displeasure," mumbled Long Barr. "She'd best go." The dwarf turned his attention to Narbie. "I'll take care of her safety, My Lady."

Helen looked at her grandmother. "I've got to go, Grandma. If it were not for Bo, I wouldn't be here right now."

Slowly facing the dwarf, she asked, "Is it going to be dangerous?"

Long Barr paused for a second and then looked at Martin.

"For Heaven's sake, Narbie," Martin sighed and shook his head. "How dangerous can applying first aid to Bo be? We'll just do that and get him back to Leachenwood." He turned back to the dwarf. "Can we get close with the automobile?"

"A bit," grumbled Long Barr, looking a bit discontented. "We'll have to leave it at Coon Creek and then walk east about two miles to the tree."

Martin cast the dwarf a grin. "You'll ride in a car?"

"Can't help it," grumbled Long Barr. He glanced at Helen and then Narbie. "The smelly thing'll save time and it's a good five miles from here to the creek bridge."

"Very good," agreed Martin as he led the others toward the old, '58 MG.

"Should I hold lunch for a bit?" asked Narbie as she walked with them.

"Uhhh," Long Barr felt of his bag. "Don't count on me, Professor. "Zee ate the last of ours about an hour ago."

"Warm the MG up, Martin," suggested Narbie and turned toward the house. "I'll put a little something in a sack for you all."

"Don't worry, Narbie," said Martin with a wave of his hand. "It's just a little jaunt down to the bridge over Coon Creek. "Bo shouldn't be far from there."

Narbie stopped and looked back at them. "You just watch that girl and be careful yourselves." Throwing a quick glance at the dwarf, she added, "The last time Helen was gone, it took a good while for her to return with those sweet potatoes, and before that, we had to call the doctor."

"We'll be just fine," assured Martin.

"Good then, but remember, we've already lost her mother

and I don't want her put in harm's way. Besides, I wasn't aware she had that many friends here." She walked past the car and on to the house.

"She's got 'em and then some," replied Martin softly.

As they approached the car, Martin leaned close to Helen and whispered, "Get in quick, child, the dwarf doesn't like cars much."

Helen looked at Long Barr as she opened the door. "Do you want in the front?"

"No. Back's safer," he replied, stepping up to and then behind the folded down seat with Zee right behind him.

Finding the key above the visor, Martin pulled the choke on the dashboard out a little, pumped the accelerator two times, inserted the key and then turned it. The motor turned over three times, backfired, and then started.

"Head for the bushes!" shouted the dwarf as he grabbed his ears and fell to the floor.

"It's all right," assured Helen as she fought back an urge to laugh.

"Don't shoot it again," Long Barr stood back up and placed his arms on the top of Helen's seat.

"Off we go," added Martin. He eased his foot off the clutch and wheeled the MG around the back of the house, sending the dwarf onto the back seats.

Lumbering down the little, paved road, the old car made short work of the five miles noted by the dwarf. As they approached the bridge, Martin eased the old car into the grass and stopped.

"Now, Belle, don't make a fuss," he said softly as he turned the key off.

Long Barr, with his hands back over his ears, smiled as the engine shuddered twice and then softly expired.

"Get out," directed the dwarf, pushing impatiently on the back of Helen's seat.

All but falling out of the back seat, Long Barr dodged the closing door, and then looked at Helen. "These things kill many people?"

"It's mostly the people who do that," quipped Helen.

"I wonder," grumbled the dwarf as he eased down the little slope from the road. "We'll go west a bit down this little path. It follows the creek all the way to the ridge where Bo's at." The dwarf slowed, looking at the dirt path more careful now. "Seleene came this direction when I scared her off Bo." He turned his attention back to Helen. "Watch Zee. They say he'll spot the wolf before we can see her."

The dwarf then stopped them right there in the trail. Shaking a light green powder in the dirt in front of each of them, he instructed, "Rub the bottom of your shoes on this but don't touch it. It'll throw the wolf off if she happens to sneak in behind us."

"I know the pepper vine berries," said Helen as she rubbed her boots over the powder, "but what is this?"

"Powdered monkshood," explained Long Barr. "It's just as good as wolfsbane. Couldn't find wolfsbane the last time I went gatherin'. It'll hide our scent, and if she licks her paws, it'll hide her as well."

"Poison," Martin explained.

Zee sniffed the innocent looking powder, sneezed, and then slowly backed away.

"Smart pup, Rosebud's got," quipped Long Barr as he took another pouch and poured out a little mound of salt next to his bit of monkshood powder. He shook a little into Helen's hand and explained. "Rock salt. Give Zee some so he won't mess with Seleene's pile. If the wolf eats it, and she'll want to, Ibenus will have to leave. That'll finish her also."

"Witches don't like salt, do they, Bo?" asked Helen.

"Nope, but if she comes back this way, it'll be a deadly distraction." He then looked at the corgi. "Check ahead for us, Zee, and come back quickly."

The orange corgi immediately turned and ran up ahead of them.

Picking up the pace at almost a run, the dwarf led Helen and her grandfather along the creek. After about thirty minutes or so, he stopped abruptly, sniffing the air like a hunting dog.

Then, without a word of explanation, he turned and whispered, "Follow me."

Noting her grandfather had his right hand in his jacket did little to comfort Helen. *After all,* she thought, *just how small is a pea shooter anyway?*

Not more than thirty paces from the creek, the dwarf stopped and looked down into the grass at his feet.

"What is it?" whispered Martin as he and Helen eased up behind him.

"Scat," answered Long Barr as he broke the stem of a knocker weed off. Trimming it up like a round-headed drumstick, he gripped the quarter-sized ball and prodded about the excrement with the shaft.

Looking back at Helen, he whispered, "Not your average bearcat. What do you see?"

Easing a bit closer to the smelly mound, she noted something dangling from the dwarf's stick. "A piece of brown fabric."

"And…" prompted the Dwarf.

"There's grass in it and it looks green."

"Good girl," said Long Barr with a smile. "We'll make a dwarf of you yet. A wolf wouldn't have left the trail to relieve itself. This is the witch's work. Seleene eats the grass because she don't feel well. I believe we're finally getting' to her."

All of a sudden, something brushed against Helen's right leg. "Geeze!" she exclaimed as she jumped and looked down at the scrub.

"It's just Zee," explained the dwarf, trying not to laugh.

"It's his way of sayin' 'hello. I'm back. Seleene's nowhere around.'" He glanced down at Zee. "Lead the way back to the trail, little friend. We must be on our way."

Now, almost at a trot again, Helen looked back at her grandfather and whispered, "How did he know all that?"

"Zee didn't bark, growl, or look out into the woods. You'll see if we get close to Seleene."

~ * ~

In just a short time later, the four came upon the rise of a high bluff that now bordered the western side of the stream and trail.

Stopping at the foot of a gradual incline, Long Barr turned to Helen and Martin. "My safe tree is at the top of this bluff." Looking back at the corgi, he instructed, "Check where Bo is hiding if you please, Zee."

The Corgi, hugging close to Helen's right leg, only stared at the dwarf for a second, and then looked directly above them and into a young red oak.

"All right then," decided the dwarf. Without another word, he spun on his heels and proceeded from the trail, toward the incline."

"Ohhh, come on Long," complained Helen, almost trotting to keep up. "I didn't catch that."

"Why not?" asked the dwarf. "Your eyes were open as were mine. What did you see?"

"Zee glanced up and then right back at you."

"Partially right can get you killed, halfling," grumbled the dwarf. Then as he turned and started up the incline. "Not up, but into that last red oak. The Fae are with us."

"Rosebud is back?" asked Helen.

"And then some," added Long Barr.

Helen immediately searched the trees. Although a good part of the morning was still with the woods, the dark shadows actually aided her. Flashes of yellow, orange, green, and red appeared here and there, moving quickly between the limbs and leaves.

"I see them. I see them," she exclaimed as she tugged on the back of Long Barr's jacket.

"That's a message, Yearling. Just seein' 'em is a gift to you." replied the dwarf. Stopping just under a haggard old oak, he turned to Helen and Martin and pulled out a black pouch from his jacket pocket. "We'll need these 'cause we didn't take the Oak Door,"

Shaking four, dime-sized, red mushrooms into the palm of his hand, he quickly ate one, tossed one to Zee, and then held the other two up for Helen and Martin.

Martin gently placed his hand on Helen's shoulder, and looked at the dwarf. "Those are redcaps, Long. Surely you know they're poisonous."

Nodding his head a bit, the dwarf replied, "Those you find in the forest truly are poison, but these little fellows were raised in the shades of Leachenwood by those who live there. They're fertilized by levistadt—the powdered remains of faerie wings. Once eaten, you'll be able to see past the Wizard Alvis's spell and hear, smell, and touch those who are there."

Helen squinted. "You mean we won't have to take the door again?"

"Didn't say that, halfling," corrected Long Barr. "This only lasts for a day or so."

"Very well, I suppose," agreed Helen.

She and her grandfather quickly ate the mushrooms.

The dwarf added, "Call to him, young one."

"We're here, aren't we," Helen said weakly as her gaze lingered on the missing top of the tree as well as the hole in its side. "Bo!" she called loudly as she ran to the opening. "Bo!" she called again. Then, ever so slowly, she peeped into the old tree.

"What kept you?" replied Bo as he groggily peeped over the side of the platform. "I've been here for days."

Martin quickly looked up into the old tree. "Rosebud, are you here?"

"Right here," she replied, sitting on the edge of the platform.

"What did you give him?" asked Martin.

"Salve made of willow bark and cure-all, and a tea with a half leaf of fox glove, just warmed good and then removed from the mix."

"That's digitalis," explained Martin. "Let's get him down quickly."

Long Barr immediately climbed the ladder and stepped onto the platform. Pulling a rope from his satchel, he formed a noose and slipped it under Bo's arms.

"Hold to the rope, Bo," he said as he scooted the dwarf close to the edge.

Stepping up the ladder a bit, Martin grabbed the rope and helped ease the dwarf to Helen's waiting arms.

"Much obliged," said Bo as his feet touched the ground.

"Take him out in the sun," instructed Martin, stepping back down the ladder. "I'll have a look at his leg."

Martin quickly followed them as Helen helped the dwarf from the tree and to the grass. Bo then sat down and pulled up the left leg of his split trousers.

"I'll be just fine," advised Bo. "But the Fae's tea's got my head spinnin' a little."

"He'll be fine," assured Rosebud. "It's not exactly my first time with the leaf. Dwarves are a lot like humans. The 'Witch's Thimble' can kill 'em easily, make 'em sick, or slow 'em down."

"I wish I had your confidence," grumbled Martin and turned

to Long Barr. "Cut two poles. We'll have to carry him."

"I'll get him a crutch," Long Barr pulled his hatchet from his belt and trotted into the woods.

Helen's gaze lingered on the tobacco pouch in Bo's hand as he smelled its contents. "I see the stem of your pipe sticking out of your vest pocket. Why don't you smoke it?"

The dwarf, shoved the pouch back into his coat pocket, frowned at the young girl. "Hold out your hand, palm down."

Slowly, Helen did what she was told.

The dwarf quickly slapped it.

"Ouch!" responded Helen and shook her hand. "What was that for?"

"Just so you'll remember," grumbled the dwarf. "Does burnin' tobacco grow in these woods?"

"Uhhh, no."

"If Seleene got a whiff of this tobacco smoke, what would she do?"

"Oh…She would come, but what of the faeries? Wouldn't they run her off?"

Helen hardly got out the words before something zipped through the air and struck her.

"Ouch!" she exclaimed, grabbing her left ear. Removing her hand, she noted a little, clear shard of a crystal in her palm. "What is this?" she asked Long Barr.

"A little bit of a step backwards, little one," replied Long Barr as he walked up, cleaning a three-foot, Y-shaped crutch for Bo. "The faes are not put off by the wolf, but Ibenus is a whole 'nother matter. Don't set 'em in harm's way if you can avoid it."

Struggling to a sitting position, Bo grumbled, "You're all wastin' time. We've got dire business to do and we need to get it done before dark. Just give me the crutch." He pulled a piece of beige, folded paper from his vest. Waving it wearily at Long Barr, he said, "I've got it."

"Got what?" asked Long Barr. Eying the paper, he dropped the crutch at Bo's side.

"A leaf from her book," responded Bo as he shook the paper for Long to take it.

"Wizard's riddle?" asked Long Barr, still not reaching for the paper.

Bo slowly nodded. "Right out of her Book of Shadows, none-theless."

Long Barr's mouth slowly opened. "Valkyrie save us," he finally said, glancing at Martin. "How'd you get it?"

"Lilly Ann, Rosebud's friend, brought it not fifteen minutes ago. Ibenus hasn't been in her house for a while and she got braver than a kicked badger."

Then, ever so slowly, Long Barr reached for the piece of folded parchment. "Up jumps the Devil, Martin." He slowly unfolded the paper.

"Hurry up, Long." Bo grabbed the crutch and pulled himself from the ground. "It's not gon'na bite you," he grumbled.

Raising a cautious eyebrow, Long Barr glanced at Bo. "Looks like it's already chewed on you some." He motioned to Helen. "Stop lookin' up in the trees for faes. Get your mind on the ground, Yearling. Seleene won't attack you from up there."

"Yes, Sir," replied Helen.

Long Barr' will do nicely, yearling. I'm not a knight."

Helen, noting the unread paper was sticking out of Long Barr's jacket pocket, eased over to him and snatched it. "I'll read it if you don't want to."

"No! No!" exclaimed Long Barr, but had little time to stop her. He shook his head in disbelief. "Go ahead. We're in this thing up to our eyeballs anyways."

"It's a poem. I think." said Helen as Bo smiled proudly.

"Riddle," corrected Long Barr.

"The Way to the Witch's Stick!" exclaimed Bo. "Read it like the dwarf Long refused to be."

Long Barr rolled his eyes, ending up on the paper in Helen's hand.

Helen looked at Long Barr's expression. Although it was troubled, he still nodded for her to continue.

Helen then read:

"Strong as Pareen, this encrusted, old friend,
did cast itself like a shadow troll
about the wood at Huntingdown's Glen.

Now leaning upon the dear one's helper
she bows her head in sweet repose,

gifted by the One who spelt her.

Ringed about with golden dills,
She hides in time within this rhyme
until the sibling's will is fulfilled."

Smiling, Bo struggled to his feet. He gestured at Martin. "Professor, we've got no time to go to Leachenwood." Bo rubbed his face briskly and then looked straight at Long Barr. "I know I'm not thinkin' clear right now, but I've been lookin' at your face while Helen read the riddle. You know somethin' 'bout what Ibenus has put in this riddle, don't you?"

"Some," responded Long Barr reluctantly.

Bo, struggling not to laughing, looked at Martin and then finally explained. "Spent some time with the witch in his younger days, he did."

"Weren't my doin'" snapped Long Barr, glancing at Martin and Helen. "She trapped me when I was just a yearling."

"'Nuff said, I suppose," stated Bo. "In this riddle, she spoke of her sister didn't she?"

"And her stick," grumbled Long Barr, throwing a quick glance at Martin. "To do what we have to do to end this, we'll have to go to Huntingdown's Glen and the Tree of Sorrows. Ethrel, I'm now quite sure, is tryin' to get the Stick of Eefron. Eefron was a gifted healer. He had one daughter—Pereen. Takin' pity on a young orphaned girl a bit older than Pereen, he adopted Ethrel." Long Barr looked at Martin and added, "Pereen is within the Tree of Sorrows, and so is her stick."

"In the tree?" asked Helen, nibbling her bottom lip as she tried to understand. "How can that be?"

Long Barr rolled his eyes and continued. "I was almost your age when Ethrel caught me. Pereen was a beautiful young, human girl of about thirty I would say. One day, while I was there, she objected to somethin' Ethrel was doin', and catchin' me didn't help matters much. Anyways, one thing led to another, and the witch tested the spell she was workin' on. Said it was perfected by Merlin. The incantation wisped Pereen from the house like smoke caught in a breeze." Long Barr nodded at Martin, "Witches brag, you know. Can't help it. I found out later that Pareen was in the old tree across from the house. She had hold of her walking stick at the time the spell was cast."

"Let's go," said Bo as he started walking down the hill toward Coon Creek. He turned his attention to Helen and Martin. "This thing has taken on a new face. It would be smart for you two to leave right now. Long and I can handle this."

Martin slowly shook his head. "We share the same enemy, old friend, but I'm worried about Helen.

"I think she is safe enough with us while we're in the woods," replied Long Barr, nodding toward Zee. "He'll let us know if trouble's near. Besides, there's the little matter of the Int."

"There's that word again," said Martin. "One day someone's going to have to explain it to me."

"None of us can," responded Bo with a chuckle. Turning to Long Barr, he asked, "Are you all right with this? Somethin's still troublin' you and I don't think it's Huntingdown's Glen."

Long slowly shook his head. "I owe a debt, but I don't care to explain it right now. We don't have the time."

Then, turning south, Helen and her grandfather followed the two dwarves. With Bo's limping, Helen knew it would be no problem keeping up.

As they stepped upon the path along Coon Creek, she eased up closer to the dwarves. "We're going to where the witch lived, aren't we?"

"Where she was allowed to stay," corrected Long Barr. "It was once the home of Eefron and Pereen Willingham." He glanced at Bo and sighed. "Everything in the first part of that riddle points to the Tree of Sorrows—it speaks of its shade as a shadow and its bark as encrusted. She then speaks of Pereen and her walkin' stick within the tree, but it's the tree that's doin' the 'bowin'. You see, the oak was huge and beautiful back then. But that's been ages ago. The spell has given it an unnatural life, but now, as every year passes, the spell weakens and the tree loses a bit of itself as it were. I can't guess what condition Pereen is in now. It is very hard to escape from that kind of a spell, even for Merlin." He glanced over at Helen. "I've been a terrible coward at best." Pausing to pull out a goose egg-sized amethyst from his pocket, he continued to speak and walk. "The last part of the riddle concerns a whole different spell I think. It speaks of a ring of 'dills'."

"I've got it!" exclaimed Bo as he all but missed a step. "There are always buttercups around that old tree. Kind o' pretty really."

"Daffodils," corrected Long Barr. "I'm hopin' to break that Faerie ring that protects Helen and the tree from the witch with this stone. Then, if we're lucky, I'm hopin' its magic will work as well on the tree...but it will come with a terrible price."

"Price?" asked Helen.

Everyone slowed, looking at Long Barr.

"'Nuff said, Yearling," said Long Barr, his voice pitched low. "If we keep pickin' at that part, I'll lose the nerve to continue. Besides, I don't fancy doin' what we have to do in the dark. Just be sure to know that Ethrel needs the Stick of Eefron to get her spirit out of the wolf, and into Pereen's body."

"But..." Helen's voice grew silent as she squinted at Long Barr. "How can she do that through the body of a wolf?"

Long Barr shrugged his shoulders as he answered, "Therein lies the ruse, Yearling. We don't yet know how. We need to free Pereen or at least destroy the stick."

"Think on it, Long," Bo picked up the pace once more, hobbling as quickly as he could. "The how is the Hobuerich."

Long Barr almost stumbled.

"There's that name again," complained Helen. "How do they keep popping up into our business?"

"All right, little one," Bo spoke as they walked on, "I'll give you a little history lesson. A long, long, time ago a great war broke out when this place was called Brittany. This was in the last days of the dragons and wizards and elves. One lesser wizard called Nimbsfork, an elf by the way, challenged a half-elf by the name of Richard Alvis for placement under the White Wizard Krypendorf. Seeing the White had chosen Alvis, Nimbsfork became hateful and jealous. He enlisted the help of a recluse clan of dark faes called the Hobuerich, meaning horrible apparition in elfin words. The war that followed cost many lives—of men, elf, fae, dwarf, and dragon alike. The great dragon Pandahar was all but killed during those times."

Long Barr took hold of Bo's arm, slowing him dramatically. "Is that why Seleene's always goin' south from Old Fiscar's place?"

"And that's where I think she is now," replied Bo.

The smile on Bo's face did little to ease Helen's discomfort as it failed to reach his eyes. Eyes that were tinged with fear. She had enough knowledge of dwarves to realize if they feared anything, it must be formidable.

So, on south the little group went with Bo struggling with his crutch, Long Barr mumbling to himself, and Zee constantly watching the woods. Finally, sometime well after noon, Bo slowed down the pace.

"Don't miss the path, Bo," warned Long Barr.

"I'm almost standin' in it," Bo grinned broadly.

Long Barr slowly shook his head as he stopped right behind Bo. "Those pasty-faced, dark daemons again," he finally grumbled. "This just keeps gettin' better 'n better."

"Yep. It will do that if we don't get to the Tree of Sorrows first," Bo added as he left the creek trail for another that could hardly be seen.

Helen, noting Long Barr wasn't moving, glanced back at her grandfather.

"That's the way to old Eefron's place," said Martin weakly.

"Well, come on Long," grumbled Bo as he paused in the path. "Five more hours and it'll be dark."

"Very well," grumbled Long Barr under his breath.

Closely following along a badly, grown-over trail, Helen could hardly see through the head-high weeds and scrub. As Bo slowed them, she noticed the remnants of a once-proud front yard. The hedge fence they were about to pass through had grown into a wall, ten feet high and at least that wide. The grass, although tended to at times, was now at her knees. Patches of buttercups thrived here and there, but the roses were struggling. Then, as she looked to her left, she stopped dead still behind the dwarves.

"Want to go in?" asked Bo with a slight smile.

Zee backed up just behind Helen and then peeped around her at the dwarf. Helen pondered the old house.

The old home, stained by Mother Nature with a grayish-green hue, still held to its faded, split-wood shingles. Although the mortar of its outside chimney was intact, it appeared to be cracked at every other stone. Its dirty windows, missing only a few panes, looked still usable, but the front porch was in ill repair. The roof leaned awkwardly to the left, giving the impression that it could go in the next stiff breeze.

Bo looked at Helen and joked again, "I didn't get an answer, Yearling. The front door is open. Do you want to see inside?"

Zee made not a sound, but watched the old house closely.

Helen slowly shook her head. "Never been inside a witch's house. I don't think I will start now."

"No need to waste time in there," Long Barr nodded to his right.

There, at the end of the front yard, stood a white oak that looked as old as time itself. With limbs that almost touched the ground, it moved silently in the breeze. Waving an abundance of green leaves, but also missing a good part of its top, it still sported a proud trunk at least six feet through its middle.

"Welcome to our world," Bo took Helen by the left arm and slowly started toward the old tree. "If your mushroom is still workin', you'll notice somethin' a little different. What do you see, little one?"

"My face and hands still tingle," she replied, watching her grandfather rub his hands also. "Does this wear off?"

"In a bit," replied Bo. "Now look toward the tree. Tell me what you see."

"There's a well-worn path to it at least three feet wide and bordered by cattails, ferns, and columbines. Butterflies are everywhere, but like none I have ever seen. Some are shades of red, others are green and blue, and there are even white and yellow ones. But they look...almost human."

"Look in the trees, Yearling," prompted Long Barr. "What do you see there?"

"There are vines in some of them with the strangest, purplish-blue flowers. They hang in clusters like grapes."

"Wisteria," Long Barr smiled. "Most beautiful flower in the woods. When the Field Faes, your butterflies, favor an old tree that's fallen on its last years, they plant the vine at its trunk. I believe they think it gives the old tree a bit of dignity in its passin'."

"Well, Bo," Martin pointedly looked around the glade, "I've been all over these woods but I don't remember this place looking anything like this."

"It's been here," assured Long Barr. "When the witch cast Merlin's spell, these Field Faes planted a flowered ring around the tree to keep Pereen and her stick, safe. The flowers still thrive."

"And so must Pereen!" exclaimed Bo. "We must hurry on while we still can!"

"This is beautiful," Helen let her hands brush over the cattails as they quickly approached the old tree.

"And so was she," Long Barr broke into a trot.

Drawing near the old oak, Helen realized its struggle was quickly becoming obvious. While the near side was green and leafy, the far side was dead and covered with every type of woodbine imaginable, especially the wisteria. When just inside the shade of the old tree, Long Barr stopped, pulled out a red bandanna from his pants pocket, and then wiped the tears from his face. Seeing emotion had taken him, Helen and the others stopped a few paces behind him.

Bo leaned in, keeping his voice low, "Let's give 'em some time, little one. He was quite fond of the human girl."

"Her struggle still exists," managed Long Barr without looking back. He cleared his throat, blew his nose, and then added, "Half eaten by sin and yet…still fightin' against it."

Helen, looking about the old tree, asked, "How is this possible? The ground looks soft and rich, the green side of the tree looks perfect, and look at those buttercups all around its base. There must be hundreds of them."

"Time for another lesson," Bo sighed. "Put your hand upon the sunny ground, lass."

Helen knelt and ran her hand through the grass and onto the soil. "It's warm and soft."

"As you are." Bo nodded and gestured to the tree. "Now, step into the shade of the old tree and do the same."

Glancing back at her grandfather, she stood and did as the dwarf requested. But as she did, she noticed Zee was reluctant to enter the shade. Looking back at her grandfather, she gently exhaled. The steam from her warm body swirled about between them as if winter.

"It's like January here." Helen shivered, rubbing her arms. "The ground is very hard."

"Keep lookin', Yearling," advised Long Barr. "Note the grass around the dills and then the flowers themselves."

Walking past Long Barr, Zee stopped her. He was barking his

disapproval. He only stopped when Bo placed his hand upon his head.

"He's just notin' the obvious, child." Long Barr patted Zee's head. "Continue, if you please."

Within four feet of the base of the tree, Helen knelt down again. "The ground is cold and the grass is frosty." She leaned forward, but as she reached into the daffodils with her right hand, the flowers broke as if glass. Quickly withdrawing her hand, she asked, "What did this? How is this possible?"

"Not yet," directed Bo as Martin started toward his grand-daughter. "Let her come to you."

Helen, slowly looking back at the three, said nothing. But the fear upon her face, and her shallow, rapid breathing, told Martin there was something terribly wrong."

"Helen!" he shouted, but was stopped once more by the stout dwarf.

"Come to us, Helen!" demanded Bo. "Do it now!"

On her knees and left hand, still holding her right close to her, she could still say or do nothing. But the silent scream from her open mouth and the tears rolling from her eyes were too much for Long Barr. Running forward, he brushed what remained of the flowers from her hand, tossed something purple into the midst of the buttercups, and then scooped Helen up into his arms. Struggling back to his feet, he ran from the shade into the sun-shine where the others were standing.

"Lay her here in the sunny grass," instructed Bo, gesturing toward a sun lit patch. "Normality's warmth will quickly chase the spell from her body."

Long Barr knelt, eased the young girl to the warm grass, and then looked up at Bo. "*Never* come this close with this child again, Bo!" he exclaimed. The scowl upon his face was proof of his an-ger.

"I was watchin', my friend. She needs to know the ways of these people," replied Bo.

Long Barr slowly stood and looked down at Helen. "I am charged with her safety, Bo, but I may need a little help."

"I'm here, old friend. Just speak it."

"If somethin' happens to me during all this, I will need you to take that charge from me."

"Done," spoke Bo as he glanced at Martin.

"What just happened?" spoke Martin, now kneeling before Helen. "She's still cold as an icicle."

"Pure, undiluted evil from Ibenus," explained Long Barr. "It's the kind you can't see until it's too late. Just rub the warmth back into her and she'll be fine."

Without another word, Long Barr stood and walked back to where Helen had knelt at the dills.

"What's he doing?" asked Martin.

"Not sure," Bo stepped to the edge of the shade.

Long Barr glanceding back. "Somethin' I should've done ages ago. I had Broderick of the Leachenwood Elves, spell a stone for me. It lies here in the dills as we speak. I should've used it much earlier, but only now have I worked up the courage to do what now needs call for."

"I was followin' your lead when we came here," said Bo as he walked toward his friend. "But now, I'm afraid of where it will take us."

"What's happening?" asked Helen. She held to Martin and struggled to stand. "Bo sounds almost scared."

"I'm not sure," admitted her grandfather, "but I believe those two are starting to do something serious."

Bo walked up beside his long-time friend and looked down at the flowers. They were thawing out and wilting all around a dark purple stone.

Now noting that Long Barr looked remarkably calm, Bo said, "Answer Helen's question, Long. I would like to know also."

Long Barr looked to Bo and smiled, "I'm just repayin' a debt long overdue, and at the same time, savin' you and the others. The Hobuerich can hear Ethrel's thoughts within Seleene's body. Considering the beast's speed, I fear that even now they are nearly here."

Long Barr, noting the breech in the faerie ring was almost complete, looked back at Helen. "I don't have time to explain it all, Yearling. When the stone completes the breech of the faerie ring, its magic will start on the tree itself…I hope." Glancing back at Bo, he continued. "Billy Bo Bumpus," his voice weakened a bit, "it's been quite an adventure, but this is where I must leave you. You have taken on a student. See that you do well with her. I'm afraid that I won't…"

Long Barr's voice then failed him and he stumbled to a sitting position in the grass.

"Long Barr! Long Barr!" screamed Bo as Helen and Martin ran to join them.

Zee, however, took not a step. He seemed to be distracted by something in the woods south of them.

Dropping his bow and quiver in the grass, Bo fell to his knees beside his old friend and grabbed the front of his shirt. As he removed Long's bow and quiver, he asked, "What have you done?"

"I…I've summoned the Valkyries, Bo," he replied. His glassy gaze never broke with his friend. "I evoked, I hope, Ethrel's last curse. I dispelled the protection of the faerie ring and exposed the Tree of Sorrows to Leachenwood's stone. I hope you might be able to drive the witch's spirit from Seleene with your arrows, but in doing so, the Hobuerich will surely kill you all. I always knew I could have freed Pareen, but I also knew the cost. For that reason, I've been a coward most of my life. But that stops right here and now."

Suddenly, something popped loudly at the base of the old tree, sending pieces of bark all about them. Long Barr, with Bo still holding to his shirt, lay back gently in the grass. Tears rolled down Bo's cheeks as he looked toward the old oak.

"Let me see," said Martin, quickly kneeling by the dwarf to check his pulse. "It's weak, but still there."

"But he's cold as ice," Bo wiped the tears from his eyes with his right jacket sleeve. He then eased the hatchet from Long Barr's belt and slipped it into his friend's hand. Looking up at Martin, Bo asked weakly, "Is there nothin' we can do?"

Slowly shaking his head, Martin replied, "This goes much deeper than any visible wound I've ever seen. I'm afraid I'm on unfamiliar ground here, Bo."

Now, with pieces of bark shattering from the old tree, they all shielded their face and fell back to the grass beside Long Barr. Helen watched as a crack slowly formed two feet from the ground on the near side of the tree. Water poured from the bottom of the rift as it widened. Two feet wide and six feet tall it quickly became. Slowly stepping forward, Helen realized the tree was revealing a young girl. A white pair of peasant shoes came into view first, then a light blue dress was uncovered. She was clutching to her chest, a burgundy, four-foot walking stick with an opaque, pearl on its top the size of a hen's egg.

"Get her out quickly, Bo," managed Long Barr. His voice weak.

Shielding his eyes from the last few pieces of bark, Bo ran to the tree, but upon getting there, feared to touch the girl.

Seeing the tree had released her and she was starting to fall, Helen ran past Bo and reached for Pereen.

"Forgive me, little one," said Bo as he stepped around Helen and grabbed Pereen just as she fell from the opening. "Take the stick," he told Helen as he struggled for a better hold on the girl.

Helen took the walking stick and then nodded toward Long Barr. "Lay her here." She pointed to the grass by Long Barr's right side.

Just as Bo eased her to the grass, a bull's horn was blown in the woods just south of them. The sound was low and vibrated through the air.

"What was that?" Helen quickly looked at Bo as Zee emitted a low, guttural growl and then backed up on the far side of Bo.

"The Hobs are here," replied Bo, almost whispering.

"And so is Seleene," added Martin as he reached into his jacket pocket.

"Hide that for now, Professor," suggested Bo as he rubbed Pereen's hands and arms. "We need to get this child awake."

"Give her a whiff of this," Martin handed the dwarf a little tube of smelling salts.

Pereen, now weekly struggling to fend off Bo, finally opened her eyes. "Where am I and who are you?" she asked the dwarf.

"Haven't forgotten me already, have you?" asked Bo.

"Bumpus?" she finally managed as she rubbed her tearing eyes to better see the dwarf. "Billy Bo?"

Bo nodded, glancing at Long Barr as he did so.

Catching that, Pareen also looked. "Ohhh, my troubled soul," she covered her mouth with her right hand. "She's killed Long Barr."

Bo quickly looked at his friend lying beside her. He was looking right at Pereen, but it was clear that the light had finally left his eyes.

"Where is Ibenus?" she asked.

"She has been killed, but her spirit is in her familiar, Seleene. Even now, she brings the Hobuerich to us."

"And they're real close right now," added Martin.

"Help me up and hand me my stick," said Pereen as she struggled to stand.

With Martin on the girl's left side and Bo on her right, Pereen slowly stood and took the Stick of Eefron as Helen offered it to her. The young girl, not much older than Helen, pushed her long blonde hair from her light blue eyes, straightened the wrinkled bodice of her dress, and then removed a small chain from her neck.

"These are Martin Tucker and Helen Durkin. They are our friends," explained Bo as he nodded to them both.

Friends are a welcomed comfort in times like these, but I hope you know what you are dealing with?" She looked at Zee. "Are the faes here?"

"Actually..." Bo glanced at Martin and Helen, "I'm not sure."

"No matter," Pereen held out her necklace to Helen. At the end of it dangled a small, silver whistle. "I don't believe I have the wind required to blow this. Will you please do it for me?"

"Very well," but when she blew it, there was no sound. Zee, however, was completely distracted by the little trinket. She tried again producing the same results. "I don't hear—"

"Shhh," hissed Pereen. "It is silent to us." She slowly turned and looked to the south. "Blow it and keep blowing it until they come."

"They?" Helen glanced at Bo. But before she could blow the whistle again, Seleene burst from the woods right where Pereen was looking. The wolf stopped when it saw Pereen barely forty paces away.

"Blow it, child! Blow it!" Bo managed to grab the corgi, he looked at Zee. "You're out matched here, boy. Just stay with us for now."

As Helen blew the silent whistle, a shadowy figure walked from the dark of the forest and stopped behind the wolf. Five feet tall it was and cloaked in a black cape with the hood up so as to keep its faced hidden.

"Look at its hands," Helen lowered her voice. "They look like the hands of a ghost."

"Certainly the right color," mocked Bo.

Watching the wolf wince every time Helen blew the whistle, the Hob finally spoke. "Ibenus," he spoke loudly but his voice was that of an old man. "How is it that the Green Witch is not contained within the tree as you said?"

Although what Ibenus said could not be heard, it obviously pleased the Hob, for he then replied, "Take care of her. We'll handle the others."

"Helen, take Zee!" exclaimed Bo as he scrambled for Long's quiver.

"Ohhh no," groaned Helen as other Hobuerich could now be seen stepping from the shadows of the woods. Being too many to count, Helen knelt by the corgi. She continued to blow the whistle much to Zee's displeasure.

"Here we go," Bo spoke weakly, putting an arrow to string.

Then, as he sighted Seleene across the top of one of Long Barr's arrows, something began to move across the field between the wolf and the forest. A smoky blur streaked from the trees, zipped across the grass, and passed so close to the cloaked figure it forced him to jump aside. Another, right behind the first, darted along the left side of the wolf, making her to stumble to the right.

"Thank the Heavens." Bo gave a long sigh, lowered his bow, and then glanced at Helen. "The Dryads are here. The Int must be close."

"It actually worked!" exclaimed Helen. She lowered the whistle, handed it back to Pereen, and then looked back at what was happening.

As if ghostly apparitions, the two shadowy figures streaked towards Helen and the others. One landed so close to Helen it made her jump. The second one shot past Helen and landed in the grass by Long Barr's left shoulder. Only when they landed could they be seen.

The fae at Helen's feet looked up at the young girl. "Not to fear, Halfling. Stand ye still."

Although female, and child-like in voice, her appearance was anything but that. Resembling teens, each of the beings had two sets of brownish, tattered looking wings, not unlike butterflies but a bit more elongated and leaf-looking. The upper, longest set, were held straight up and the lower ones close to the calves of their legs. The edges of their long shirts and calf-length trousers were cut and dyed to resemble the edges of the oak leaf.

Helen, looking down at her, managed only a weak, "Thank you."

Ignoring the Hobuerich, the one next to Helen lowered her upper wings to her back like a wasp. She then directed her words at Pereen. "Daughter of Eefron, approach the wolf and call the light."

"What?" Bo faced Pereen. "Can you do this?"

Pereen frowned at the Dryad. "What of the dark one near him?"

"Fear not, youngling. The Int is near and we are many."

Pereen turned her attention to Bo. "I know the words. I think I can do this. My father said faith is all I would need."

Bracing herself on every step with her walking stick, she left Martin and Bo and started toward the wolf. Seleene's hackles rose as she slowly bared her teeth.

"No!" said Helen loudly to Zee. She all but hugged the strong corgi to keep him from charging the wolf.

Eight more Dryads shot from the forest above the other Hobuerichs, causing the single Hob close to Seleene to give ground and edge toward the others nearer the trees. The shadowy figures of the Dryads flew about the wolf in a twelve-foot circle and then landed in the grass all around her. Seleene, although still showing anger, remained still and eyed the young girl as she approached.

"Illustro," spoke Pereen softly as she neared the circle.

The young girl tapped the ground three times with the base of the walking stick. A blinding light exploded from the opaque crystal causing the wolf to cringe and lower her head. The Hobuerich, however, had no intention of standing still. Although they didn't leave, they backed well within the shadows of the forest save the one by himself. He gave ground, but remained in the open.

Now, within one step of the Dryad ring, Pereen stopped and looked at the wolf. "Your spell killed my friend, Long Barr, Ethrel." Although her voice and body seemed weak, the anger in her eyes gave lie to the appearance. "He gave his life to save me and the others."

Even though she spoke softly, there was little doubt she was seething in anger.

"Come out of the wolf!" shouted Pereen. She stepped through the ring of Dryads, holding the Staff of Eefron above her.

Closing its eyes, the wolf lowered its head against the blinding light. Finally, as all watched, a dark figure peeled itself through the animal's fir and from its body as so much dead skin. Settling upon the grass at the wolf's right side and with nowhere to go, the apparition rose, taking on the darkened silhouette of Ibenus. Then, as a silent scream shaped the figure's mouth, the wolf wheeled, ran through the Dryad ring, and then disappeared into the forest.

"Die, witch," commanded Pereen loudly. The figure melted into the grass like a meadow's fog on a warm morning.

"Decresco," whispered Pereen, causing the light upon the staff's head to fade.

"Well done," said the Dryad at Helen's feet. The fae moved swiftly, approaching the Hob still in the open. Hovering only a few feet from his hooded face, she said, "We have you out numbered ten to one Dark One. The Black Witch no longer exists.

Go back to the yellow grass and do not return."

In silence the Hob backed from the Dryad and disappeared into the shadows of the forest. Pereen, seeing that the Dryad was still close to Long Barr, hurried toward the two.

Bo smiled as she approached and nodded toward the fae at Long's shoulder. "Our friend says he sleeps."

"Nay! Witchen slumber, Bo," corrected the Dryad. "No return for him. He'll nare last the week, daughter of Eefron." The Dryad then stepped away from Long Barr and bit closer to Pereen. "Do you know 'The Words that Bind?'"

That phrase struck Pereen like a dagger through her heart. All the emotions the present circumstances had refused to show, suddenly proved overwhelming. Dropping her stick to the grass, she ran to Long Barr's side, and collapsed to her knees with her face in her hands.

"I can't. I just can't," she sobbed. "It seems only yesterday I was talking to him. Now this."

Bo, kneeling beside her kept his voice soft as he explained, "There's no way to keep him but this, young one." He also wiped his eyes. "He will be with the Ints and they will take care of him. They are Druids and will not fail him."

"That's true, Green One," agreed the Dryad. "The Valkyries will not be sent for him. And as long as you remember, he will visit you in your dreams."

Pereen looked up at Bo. "Is that his only hope?"

The dwarf, saying not a word, wiped his eyes and slowly nodded.

"Very well...I will do this thing."

The Dryads, now streaming from the forest, looked indeed uncountable. As they settled to the grass about the old tree,

Helen whispered to Bo, "What spectacle is this?"

"Watch and learn, Yearling. Watch and learn."

The chatter among the Dryads quickly grew silent as every eye turned to the one they considered to be a Green Witch.

Now, leaning close to her, Bo said, "Do it while breath is still in him."

Pereen wiped her eyes, placed her hand upon Long Barr's chest, and then spoke the spell.

"With the patience of a stone,
and the happiness of a Sprite,
thou wilt remain in this oak content
as a mushroom on a warm Sumer's night."

"Holliock!" she fell back into the grass at Bo's feet.

As Bo tended to Pereen, Helen watched the wind begin to stir. First the cold from the north came, swirling the grass all about them. Then, from the south, blew a warm breeze to mingle with the cold.

"Hold to me," said Martin. He grabbed Helen and pulled her close.

Around and around it blew, gathering leaves from the nearby trees as it went. As others closed their eyes and turned away, Helen remained determined to see yet another happening. With leaves and grass stinging her face and arms, she watched as a darkened cyclone formed over Long Barr causing Bo and Pereen to move back with them. Then, little by little, it hid him from sight.

"It's got him! It's got him!" exclaimed Pereen as she clung to Bo.

Helen closed her eyes, gasped, and held to her grandfather's arm. Glancing toward the old tree, she glimpsed the leafy cyclone as it moved into the midst of it, causing its limbs to move about wildly, putting the Dryads to flight.

Trying to hide her face once more, she felt her grandfather nudged her. "Better look at this, Helen. The storm has changed the old oak."

"Ohhh my," said Helen weakly as she looked at what was now a stronger and much younger tree.

Close to a hundred feet it was now. Missing not a limb, it stood, young and proud. Three feet through the trunk, it appeared to be thick with leaves.

"It's perfect." Helen slowly stood with the others. "Hasn't got a mark on it."

"You're wrong," disagreed Bo.

The dwarf pointed to the base of the tree. There, roughly a foot from the ground started a perfectly smooth scar, one-foot-wide and five-feet-tall.

"Pereen's charm has allowed Long's life force to heal the oak," explained Bo as the Dryads cheered. "Now it's young and virile again." The dwarf then looked up at Pereen. "The Ints have him now, My Lady. When the oak finally washes the spell from his body, they will let him move about this forest like a great owl and you'll never be lonely again."

About the Author

Greetings from Camelot Cove:

After retiring from 'Ma Bell' in the year 1999, I seriously took to the pen. Through E-Bay and various bookstores, my novel collection, *The Pragamore Chronicles*, eventually reached more than eight countries.

My poetry has won the Editor's Choice Awards from the International Library of Poetry in 1999, 2000, and 2002. *View from the Easley Place*, a short story, is on exhibition at Munford Library. My stories are published in such anthologies as Clockwork Spells and Magical Bells ('Quest for the Dragon Scale-Kerlak), ParAABnormal ('Spotter'-Sam's Dot), Stories in the Ether ('Shelled'-Nevermet), 'Unlikely Friend' (Sam's Dot), and 'Apprentice' (Sam's Dot).

Added short story features include, 'Hell's Gate' (Seven Star Press), and 'Phagan's Shadow' (WolfSinger). Coming short stories are 'Cry Wolf' with Dark Oak and 'The Ghost of Queen Anne's Revenge' also with Dark Oak. On the front burners in 2015, are the novellas, 'The Curse of the Monkey's Paw' with Tyree Campbell and his Alban Lake Publishing and 'The Angel of Holloway' from Tommy Hancock and ProSe Productions.

In the works are novellas, 'In the Shadows of the White Owls (Held by Under the Moon), 'Bedouin', 'The Angel of Holloway', 'Ooze', and 'The Moleskin Cap' with WolfSinger.

The year 2016 promises to be a 'One-Of-A-Kind'. It starts out with the publishing two, novellas, two large short stories, and then sours from there.

Keep reading and I'll keep writhing…

M. R. Williamson
mwilli44@comcast.net
pragamorechronicles.com
Imagicopter.com

More magical adventures available from WolfSinger Publications

The City Under the Bridge – Laura J. Underwood

When Anwyn Baldomyre stumbled upon Stonegorge, he was fascinated to find an entire city built under a bridge. But the moment he stepped under its tall arches seeking shelter for the night, he knew something was amiss. Stonegorge was being ravaged by the rising river that threatened to wash its foundations away, as well as a frightening creature the locals call The Water Lady, a creature who drowns men on dry land.

Soon, the river will tear out the foundations of the bridge if nothing is done. So Anwyn embarks on solving the mystery of the Water Lady and seeing what he can do to help the folk who live at the base of the bridge known as The Depths. But there are those who would just as soon the Harper Mage not learn the truth, for that would spoil their plans to run those who dwell in The Depths from their homes and put the wealth of Stonegorge into their own pockets.

But silver eyes and a golden voice and magic songs may not be enough to save The City Under the Bridge unless Anwyn can solve the riddles buried in Stonegorge itself.

Demonsword – Dan Devine

Paul has only known Jack Allister for a little over a week when two strange men show up at the inn looking for his new friend. As the innkeeper's son bravely seeks to warn Jack, Paul soon finds himself caught up in an epic quest to stop the second coming of the evil god Arzak.

A month ago, Jack was nothing but a humble farm boy but he now finds himself chosen by the magical Demonsword Cartos to wield it in the coming war. Even worse, Jack finds himself with uncertain allies; as the cult of wizards that brought him to the sword seek only to control him, while some of the other chosen warriors will use their Demonswords to betray him in an attempt to save themselves rather than the world in which they live.

With the forces of good in such disarray, the Earth seems doomed, until Paul is unexpectedly anointed as the spokesman for humanity's patron god Paytr. The young boy must grow up fast and put his fears and his uncertainty behind him as he fights with his friend against black magic on his way into the desolate domain of the dark god himself. In the end it is young Paul, not the other heroes, who must face Arzak alone and use his faith and his god's magic to defeat him and save everything that he holds dear.

Fanny & Dice – Rebecca McFarland Kyle

"I'm leaving Hell for good, Eurydice…"

When she heard those words, Eurydice had a choice: remain in Hades' realm or escape to Earth with her kinswoman, Persephone.

She knew the Earth wasn't what they'd left. Demeter hadn't summoned Persephone to bring Spring for quite some time…and the last dead crossed the River Styx many years before.

She hadn't expected to arrive in a world where trains rode across the prairie on metal tracks instead of chariots and men settled disputes with six guns instead of swords.

Eurydice will face perils both immortal and mortal, from gun and axe to her own heart.….

The King's Champion – M.H. Bonham

For over fifty years, fireworms have ravaged the city of Citadel Heights. Warriors and wizards have sought to find the answer to the attacks, but to little avail. Each raid has decimated the Chi'lan warriors, the elite guard of King Romarin, the son of Rhyn'athel, the warrior god.

Kalena, a young squire to Cahal, the King's Champion, knows all too well the peril that the fireworms bring. As she watches her friends and fellow warriors die in the attacks, she knows something must be done. A tragic loss sends her on a quest with Romarin, himself, to find the source of the attacks and to perform daring rescue. But an ancient evil lurks in the fireworms lair that even the magic of Romarin may not be able to fight, and forces Kalena to face an enemy even more dangerous than the fireworms…

Maya, Resurrected – Kimberly Todd Wade

859 A.D. Yohl Ik'nal ("Heart of the Wind Place") is alone with her two starving children on their drought-stricken farm. Her husband and two grown sons have been drafted to fight in a distant war. Will they ever return? Yohl can't afford to wait. Her hungry children must be fed. It's time to dig up Yohl's past, for her mother was a princess, her grandfather a king. She still has relatives amongst the Maya royalty. They are her best hope for salvation.

Follow Yohl and her children as they travel Maya causeways, highways of the ancient world, through ravaged jungle and depressed homesteads to the capital city, itself on the verge of economic collapse. Can the religious spectacle of human sacrifice provoke the Gods' beneficence? If the Maya ceremonies and myths fail, Yohl has recourse to the older, deeper traditions of the forest people. She'll do whatever necessary to survive.